RICH PRIDE

FROM A CRYING CUB TO A ROARING LION

M. L. MOORE

RICH PRIDE

Copyright © 2018 M. L. Moore

Printed in the United States of America

ISBN: 978-0-9992646-2-1

HOW TO READ THIS BOOK

We suggest you read this book in two parts. First read about Rich Pride, and then read the speeches on the side.

This book is not policy for Rich Pride. The ideas inside can be approved or modified as we ascertain what our members won't, and the best course of action to take and building our community.

CHAPTER 1

"No one in this world dare deny that America's wealth and power stemmed from 310 years of slave labor contributed from the American so-called negro."
—**Malcom X.**

I used to believe that racism was behind us. But as you can see from what's transpiring around the country, that's far from authentic.

If you watch the news, you see white mobs walk around with Nazi flags, as if it's the 1940's.

There are white militia prepared for war.

They train with firearm; learning how to protect their people, in case of a race war.

We have a president who took days to denounce the KKK, and once he did he defined them.

Our president is a racist, and he never keeps it a secret..

So as much as we want to manipulate the reality of things, it's still present today.

If a race war happened today, what would blacks do to protect themselves?

What organizations other than the U.S government do we have to defend us?

What money, land, or any other assets do we own? None. The black race in America doesn't own anything as a body.

Now there are individuals in our community that are rich, and can afford security. But what is the fate of the poor? Who's going to protect them?

have never been just a collection of individuals or a collection of red states and blue states.

We are, and always will be, the United States of America.

It's the answer that led those who've been told for so long by so many to be cynical and fearful and doubtful about what we can achieve to put their hands on the arc of history and bend it once more toward the hope of a better day.

It's been a long time coming, but tonight, because of what we did on this date in this election at this defining moment change has come to America.

A little bit earlier this evening, I received an extraordinarily gracious call from Sen. McCain.

Sen. McCain fought long and hard in this campaign. And he's fought even longer and harder for the country that he loves. He has endured sacrifices for America that most of us cannot begin to imagine. We are better off for the service rendered by this brave and selfless leader.

I congratulate him; I congratulate Gov. Palin for all that they've achieved. And I look forward to working with them to renew this nation's promise in the months ahead.

I want to thank my partner in this journey, a man who campaigned from his heart, and spoke for the men and women he grew up with on the streets of Scranton and rode with on the train home to Delaware, the vice president-elect of the United States, Joe Biden.

And I would not be standing here tonight without the unyielding support of my best friend for the last 16 years the rock of our family, the love of my life, the nation's next first lady Michelle Obama. Sasha and Malia I love you both more than you can imagine. And you have earned the new puppy that's coming with us to the new White House.

I know the chances of a race war happening is slim to none, because for every racist in this country there are 5 to 10 other people who aren't.

The race war example was a worst-case illustration. Its purpose was to demonstrate how unprepared we are, and how far behind we are from other races.

The black race is probably the less organized race on earth.

We are not focused on the future and can't seem to come together. There is a lot of hatred among us, and there is no support.

Most blacks don't support black owned businesses, and there are a lot of loss brothers and sisters out there.

In over a hundred years, we haven't been able to mobilize and build a long-lasting mass movement. This is not because of laziness, here are great leaders from the civil rights movement who gave their lives in pursuit of a brighter future for our people.

But after that battle was won for civil rights, things began to collapse. We became contented with yesterday's glory. We stopped the marches and started using drugs. The crack epidemic set us back decades.

If you think about it a moment, where were our people headed before drugs ravaged our community?

I'll tell you! We were building an empire, that which would've changed the future.

But once drugs hit it all came to an end.

Parents, who were supposed to be home raising their children, were out booting and chasing their next high.

And while she's no longer with us, I know my grandmother's watching, along with the family that made me who I am. I miss them tonight. I know that my debt to them is beyond measure.

To my sister Maya, my sister Alma, all my other brothers and sisters, thank you so much for all the support that you've given me. I am grateful to them.

And to my campaign manager, David Plouffe, the unsung hero of this campaign, who built the best — the best political campaign, I think, in the history of the United States of America.

To my chief strategist David Axelrod who's been a partner with me every step of the way.

To the best campaign team ever assembled in the history of politics you made this happen, and I am forever grateful for what you've sacrificed to get it done.

But above all, I will never forget who this victory truly belongs to. It belongs to you. It belongs to you.

I was never the likeliest candidate for this office. We didn't start with much money or many endorsements. Our campaign was not hatched in the halls of Washington. It began in the backyards of Des Moines and the living rooms of Concord and the front porches of Charleston. It was built by working men and women who dug into what little savings they had to give $5 and $10 and $20 to the cause.

It grew strength from the young people who rejected the myth of their generation's apathy who left their homes and their families for jobs that offered little pay and less sleep.

It drew strength from the not-so-young people who braved the bitter cold and scorching heat to knock on doors of perfect strangers, and from the millions of Americans who volunteered and organized and proved that more than two centuries later

When they should be at home molding our future leaders. But the use of these drugs was only half the problem. The black man began to sell these drugs, and was very desperate to free himself from poverty, only to end up behind bars.

He never thought about what his absence would do to his family, how much it would affect their way of living, and how not having a father would hurt the kid's upbringing.

With so many fathers, incarcerated mothers were left to feed their family alone.

If you ask me, I believe the drug epidemic starting in the 60's is to blame for the condition our people are in today.

CHAPTER 2

"No one is more innocent then the poor, blind American so-called Negro who has been led astray by blind Negro leaders."
—**Malcom X**

Rich pride is a tribe. Its goal is to help build the black race and help our economy. We strive to build our community wealth, and social power in influence.

Rich Pride will fight for its independence from America. We want to build our own state, and have our own political identity, banks, and army.

We know that America is a great country but wish to have our independence to form a black state with our own businesses, taxes, banks, and land, within this country.

a government of the people, by the people, and for the people has not perished from the Earth.

This is your victory.

And I know you didn't do this just to win an election. And I know you didn't do it for me.

You did it because you understand the enormity of the task that lies ahead. For even as we celebrate tonight, we know the challenges that tomorrow will bring are the greatest of our lifetime — two wars, a planet in peril, the worst financial crisis in a century.

Even as we stand here tonight, we know there are brave Americans waking up in the deserts of Iraq and the mountains of Afghanistan to risk their lives for us.

There are mothers and fathers who will lie awake after the children fall asleep and wonder how they'll make the mortgage or pay their doctors' bills or save enough for their child's college education.

There's new energy to harness, new jobs to be created, new schools to build, and threats to meet, alliances to repair.

The road ahead will be long. Our climb will be steep. We may not get there in one year or even in one term. But, America, I have never been more hopeful than I am tonight that we will get there.

I promise you, we as a people will get there.

There will be setbacks and false starts. There are many who won't agree with every decision or policy I make as president. And we know the government can't solve every problem.

But I will always be honest with you about the challenges we face. I will listen to you, especially when we disagree. And, above all, I will ask you to join in the work of remaking this nation, the only way it's been done in America for 221 years — block by block, brick by brick, calloused hand by calloused hand.

We want it to be clear that we are not a racist organization, but we are pro black.

We believe in the right to bear arms.

Rich Pride understands the exploitation and oppression of people, the injustice and inequality of the system of government under which the white minority has subjugated the African American people.

Our goal is to take a little time away from protest. Because after 50 years of nonviolent protest by blacks against whites, so many has failed to bring meaningful reform and instead to prompt working on economic resources, by coming together to buy businesses and land to call our own.

It will take time to get people to believe we can come together and invest our money into something without greed getting in the way.

We understand because the black enterprise has been held back by human materialism, thirst, and ambition for decades.

But we're passionate about our future and will be transparent when it comes to financing our businesses. The profits will go to members and to assembling our tribe.

The future member family won't have to wage an exhausting struggle against poverty, disease, and unemployment to pay their rent and to put food on the table.

When we own our own businesses, members in need of employment will be given a job.

Rich Pride will be an honest empire, a place where people play apart in the decision process. Our

What began 21 months ago in the depths of winter cannot end on this autumn night.

This victory alone is not the change we seek. It is only the chance for us to make that change. And that cannot happen if we go back to the way things were.

It can't happen without you, without a new spirit of service, a new spirit of sacrifice.

So let us summon a new spirit of patriotism, of responsibility, where each of us resolves to pitch in and work harder and look after not only ourselves but each other.

Let us remember that, if this financial crisis taught us anything, it's that we cannot have a thriving Wall Street while Main Street suffers.

In this country, we rise or fall as one nation, as one people. Let's resist the temptation to fall back on the same partisanship and pettiness and immaturity that has poisoned our politics for so long.

Let's remember that it was a man from this state who first carried the banner of the Republican Party to the White House, a party founded on the values of self-reliance and individual liberty and national unity.

Those are values that we all share. And while the Democratic Party has won a great victory tonight, we do so with a measure of humility and determination to heal the divides that have held back our progress.

As Lincoln said to a nation far more divided than ours, we are not enemies but friends. Though passion may have strained, it must not break our bonds of affection.

And to those Americans whose support I have yet to earn, I may not have won your vote tonight, but I hear your voices. I need your help. And I will be your president, too.

And to all those watching tonight from members will help decide our future.

We won't over extend our membership and will only allow new members in once a year. We plan to manage memberships to prevent over extending our financial resources.

Rich Pride wants every member to be able to find work. We want our unemployment rate to be 0%

All business will be members' own, and profit will be distributed amongst all members.

Our goal is to own our own land, where members will live — housing will be made affordable.

To become a part of Rich Pride, you must be willing to invest in your future and the future of the tribe.

CHAPTER 3

"Black men have always been wise, black men have always been the wisest beings in the universe."
—Malcom X

A lot of black people are a part of gangs, and worship the leaders of these gangs.

I want to ask all gang members younger than 40 years old, what have these leaders done for you?

How many love ones have you lost for colors? And for the love you have for a leader, you will never meet.

Blacks kill each other and spend time behind bars, where most of their friends and fellow gang members forget about them.

It's my understanding that most street individuals believe they

beyond our shores, from parliaments and palaces, to those who are huddled around radios in the forgotten corners of the world, our stories are singular, but our destiny is shared, and a new dawn of American leadership is at hand.

To those — to those who would tear the world down: We will defeat you. To those who seek peace and security: We support you. And to all those who have wondered if America's beacon still burns as bright: Tonight we proved once more that the true strength of our nation comes not from the might of our arms or the scale of our wealth, but from the enduring power of our ideals: democracy, liberty, opportunity and unyielding hope.

That's the true genius of America: that America can change. Our union can be perfected. What we've already achieved gives us hope for what we can and must achieve tomorrow.

This election had many firsts and many stories

that will be told for generations. But one that's on my mind tonight's about a woman who cast her ballot in Atlanta. She's a lot like the millions of others who stood in line to make their voice heard in this election except for one thing: Ann Nixon Cooper is 106 years old.

She was born just a generation past slavery; a time when there were no cars on the road or planes in the sky; when someone like her couldn't vote for two reasons — because she was a woman and because of the color of her skin.

And tonight, I think about all that she's seen throughout her century in America — the heartache and the hope; the struggle and the progress; the times we were told that we can't, and the people who pressed on with that American creed: Yes we can.

At a time when women's voices were silenced and their hopes dismissed, she lived to see them

are intelligent. That's why I can't comprehend how they don't see being a part of a gang is meaningless today. Gangs are not the same as they were back in the days. There is no loyalty, no plan, and no future in gang banging.

I just wanted to point that out. But it isn't the business of the pride to dictate the way our members live.

At the same time, we require all members to be loyal to the tribe and the future of our people over everything.

We do not want people who are not open minded and don't have a vision. There is no place in the tribe for people who believe they are too cool to participate in the movement.

We are not like some of the movements in the past that wanted to change how you live your life. The only thing we wish to change is your financial status.

There is no plan to force black people to act like any other race.

We will still live life the way we do today. We will still party and do the things that are a part of our culture. The only thing that will change is how we ball. It will be on another level, every member will be paid, and well off.

Rich Pride will have one of the best economy this world has ever seen. We will build our people up from the ground, and just under 20 years.

The people who joined the tribe from the beginning will still be alive to reap the reward.

We must change now, we can't still be last a hundred years from now.

stand up and speak out and reach for the ballot. Yes we can.

When there was despair in the dust bowl and depression across the land, she saw a nation conquer fear itself with a New Deal, new jobs, a new sense of common purpose. Yes we can.

When the bombs fell on our harbor and tyranny threatened the world, she was there to witness a generation rise to greatness and a democracy was saved. Yes we can.

She was there for the buses in Montgomery, the hoses in Birmingham, a bridge in Selma, and a preacher from Atlanta who told a people that "We Shall Overcome." Yes we can.

A man touched down on the moon, a wall came down in Berlin, a world was connected by our own science and imagination.

And this year, in this election, she touched her finger to a screen, and cast her vote, because after 106 years in America, through the best of times and the darkest of hours, she knows how America can change.

Yes we can.

America, we have come so far. We have seen so much. But there is so much more to do. So tonight, let us ask ourselves — if our children should live to see the next century; if my daughters should be so lucky to live as long as Ann Nixon Cooper, what change will they see? What progress will we have made?

This is our chance to answer that call. This is our moment.

This is our time, to put our people back to work and open doors of opportunity for our kids; to restore prosperity and promote the cause of peace; to reclaim the American dream and reaffirm that fundamental truth, that, out of many, we are one; that while we breathe, we hope. And where we are met with cynicism and doubts and those who tell us that we can't, we will respond with

We have opportunities available today that weren't available 50 years ago.

There are no more excuses, the time for change is now.

Real freedom is participation in power.

We are ready to change the world, and change the future. But we need people who want real "Freedom."

We need people who want power, money, and a family. One that will invest in our future and the future of our people.

The black race won't be respected until we start respecting ourselves. More so, we will never respect ourselves until we have the means to live respectably.

The first black republic was established in 1804, and Haitians.

Rich Pride was established 4/19/2016. We understand there will be an up-hill battle, and that there will be people who don't believe our vision is possible.

There are going to be individuals who will laugh at us, and try to oppress our ambition, but a hundred years from today, we will own the future. They will mention Rich Pride name with Great Nations.

Our day of independence will come. We can't afford to be left behind anymore, on any level.

People will call us racists, which we are not, because racism is a product of ignorance and a host of other factors: selfishness, arrogance, aggression, and greed.

What is racism? The dogma that one ethic group is condemned by nature to be hereditary inferior? What is the logical conclusion? Genocide.

that timeless creed that sums up the spirit of a people: Yes, we can.

Although I love "Obama" in agree that America is the best nation in the world now, but still I must remind the people that there is always a nation waiting to be greater. Mary Mclead Bethune said these great words. "And I stand by them. "Now I speak, Mr. President, not as Mrs. Bethune but as the voice of fourteen million Americans who seek to achieve full citizenship. We have been taking the crumbs for a long time we have been eating the feet and hand of the chicken long enough. The time has come when we want some white meat. There is no place in business, no other place in government where we can go where we feel like we really belong, really have a contribution to make. The further an individual is down, the more chance he has to come up. But the negro cannot find his way to the opportunities that are opening unless he have someone to guide him." We the people of Rich Pride will guide each other outta poverty. I want you to read these next speeches in tell me if all the problems have been solved. Now don't get me wrong some have! But they all tell a story of some that still remain today. All you gotta do is read in you'll see that some of the problems we faced 60 years ago still remain in wont be fixed until we fix them.

"GIVE US THE BALLOT," ADDRESS AT THE PRAYER PILGRIMAGE FOR FREEDOM.

Mr. Chairman, distinguished platform associates, fellow Americans. Three years ago the Supreme Court of this nation rendered in simple, eloquent, and unequivocal language a decision which will long be stenciled on the mental sheets of succeeding generations. For all men of goodwill, this May seventeenth decision came as a joyous daybreak to end

We don't plan to hurt anyone, we don't believe we're better than another race.

Our goals are to protect our people, and to rebuild the economic status of blacks. Because if we don't, who will?

Having a family heritage to live up to is an incentive for whites, and not having one has made achievement more difficult for blacks in failure easier to accept. We plan to change that.

We are starting now, so that a hundred years from now our kids will have a heritage rich with pride and achievements, that which will give them a balanced life, where they have time to seek things for the mind in spirit.

We plan to make money in plenty of it. Because today, what we call money is only stored labor.

Most of us work our asses off only to be able to buy what's necessary. But a hundred years from now our kids will live the lives of kings and queens.

They will have knowledge in power, not just academic knowledge but awareness of how to do things.

Our kids will have both money and education, and a land to call their own. They won't have to worry about discrimination or denial of their rights.

Our future is bright, if we come together.

If we can't then the rest of our existence will be spent at the bottom.

Other races will look on our people in grasp what not to do.

I don't know about you, but I can't stand for this. I don't want the long night of human captivity. It came as a great beacon light of hope to millions of disinherited people throughout the world who had dared only to dream of freedom.

Unfortunately, this noble and sublime decision has not gone without opposition. This opposition has often risen to ominous proportions. Many states have risen up in open defiance. The legislative halls of the South ring loud with such words as "interposition" and "nullification."

But even more, all types of conniving methods are still being used to prevent Negroes from becoming registered voters. The denial of this sacred right is a tragic betrayal of the highest mandates of our democratic tradition. And so our most urgent request to the president of the United States and every member of Congress is to give us the right to vote. [*Audience:*] (*Yes*)

Give us the ballot, and we will no longer have to worry the federal government about our basic rights.

Give us the ballot (*Yes*), and we will no longer plead to the federal government for passage of an anti-lynching law; we will by the power of our vote write the law on the statute books of the South (*All right*) and bring an end to the dastardly acts of the hooded perpetrators of violence.

Give us the ballot (*Give us the ballot*), and we will transform the salient misdeeds of bloodthirsty mobs (*Yeah*) into the calculated good deeds of orderly citizens.

Give us the ballot (*Give us the ballot*), and we will fill our legislative halls with men of goodwill (*All right now*) and send to the sacred halls of Congress men who will not sign a "Southern Manifesto" because of their devotion to the manifesto of justice. (*Tell 'em about it*) Give us the ballot (*Yeah*),

to have to worry about my kids being gunned down by police.

I've seen enough black men killed by officers, and the world watched it like it's nothing. This only happens because we are poor and don't stand up for each other.

How many times have you watched an unarmed black man gunned down and cold blood, only to witness the officer set free.

I know people are seeing more of this today, because cameras are everywhere, and people are recording it. But it's nothing new.

What's crazy is that even with cameras the system is letting it play out the same.

These officers are being let off, because they know we won't come together. They know most of us will only get mad for a day or two, before moving on.

If we had a system of our own to fight back it would stop.

What if we had lawyers, whose job would be to define our members no matter what the system claims they are guilty of.

Rich pride will stand up for our people to make sure they don't get killed, or rail roaded by a system that has no problem putting them away.

This system is created to beat down the poor, white or black it doesn't matter your color. But black people must fight against laws created when racist ran this country.

This is something everyone knows, but no one wants to change these laws, that were made to hold us back.

That's why we need to buy our own land, a place that will keep us safe from anyone planning to and we will place judges on the benches of the South who will do justly and love mercy (*Yeah*), and we will place at the head of the southern states governors who will, who have felt not only the tang of the human, but the glow of the Divine.

Give us the ballot (*Yes*), and we will quietly and nonviolently, without rancor or bitterness, implement the Supreme Court's decision of May seventeenth, 1954. (*That's right*) In this juncture of our nation's history, there is an urgent need for dedicated and courageous leadership. If we are to solve the problems ahead and make racial justice a reality, this leadership must be fourfold.

First, there is need for strong, aggressive leadership from the federal government. So far, only the judicial branch of the government has evinced this quality of leadership. If the executive and legislative branches of the government were as concerned about the protection of our citizenship rights as the federal courts have been, then the transition from a segregated to an integrated society would be infinitely smoother. But we so often look to Washington in vain for this concern. In the midst of the tragic breakdown of law and order, the executive branch of the government is all too silent and apathetic. In the midst of the desperate need for civil rights legislation, the legislative branch of the government is all too stagnant and hypocritical.

This dearth of positive leadership from the federal government is not confined to one particular political party. Both political parties have betrayed the cause of justice. (*Oh yes*) The Democrats have betrayed it by capitulating to the prejudices and undemocratic practices of the southern Dixiecrats.

harm us, and we can't be racially profiled.

I know this may seem impossible now, but it is possible. Rome wasn't built over night, and anything that's worth having takes time and challenging work.

Our people have been programmed to be okay with, where we stand in this world for decades.

But now it's time we think on our own, now is the time to free your mind of bad ideas that were planted there.

There's never been a better time to become a part of a movement that will change the world.

A movement that in a hundred years will own the world. One that will change how other races view the black race.

A movement that's going to transform us back to the kings and queens we once were.

We need your help changing the world. Become a member of Rich Pride and become a part of black history.

Rich Pride is nothing like any other organization in the world. We are not money hungry and don't seek to change the life of one individual, but to change the life of every member.

We don't want to spend time talking about how we have been mistreated. No. We want to change the way we're being treated.

We are prepared to be called racists, and for people to laugh at our plans.

But we want them to know we are revolutionaries and won't let haters stop us.

The Republicans have betrayed it by capitulating to the blatant hypocrisy of right wing, reactionary northerners. These men so often have a high blood pressure of words and an anemia of deeds. [*laughter*]

In the midst of these prevailing conditions, we come to Washington today pleading with the president and members of Congress to provide a strong, moral, and courageous leadership for a situation that cannot permanently be evaded. We come humbly to say to the men in the forefront of our government that the civil rights issue is not an ephemeral, evanescent domestic issue that can be kicked about by reactionary guardians of the status quo; it is rather an eternal moral issue which may well determine the destiny of our nation (*Yeah*) in the ideological struggle with communism. The hour is late. The clock of destiny is ticking out.

We must act now, before it is too late.

A second area in which there is need for strong leadership is from the white northern liberals. There is a dire need today for a liberalism which is truly liberal. What we are witnessing today in so many northern communities is a sort of quasi-liberalism which is based on the principle of looking sympathetically at all sides. It is a liberalism so bent on seeing all sides, that it fails to become committed to either side. It is a liberalism that is so objectively analytical that it is not subjectively committed. It is a liberalism which is neither hot nor cold, but lukewarm. (*All right*) We call for a liberalism from the North which will be thoroughly committed to the ideal of racial justice and will not be deterred by the propaganda and subtle words of those who say: "Slow up for a while; you're pushing too fast."

CHAPTER 4

"For four hundred years America has been a wolf's den for twenty million so-called Negroes twenty million second-class citizens."
—**Malcom X**

Back in the days, whites believed it was affirmed that the negro could not take care of themselves.

What's crazy about this statement is slaves spent their time taking care of whites. I can't understand how they came up with this conclusion, when blacks were able to take care of them.

I'm here to say, I know we can take care of ourselves, and it's time we have an organization that will do this.

Rich Pride won't use the US government for banking. Our

currency will be bitcoin, which I'm passionate about, because it is one of the most exciting inventions of the last decades. It's a platform for building decentralized trusted applications for financial services, commerce and governance.

The financial freedom that bitcoin will provide will be as revolutionary as the educational and informational freedom provided by the internet.

We will gain the economic freedom that will enable us to climb the economic ladder in a way we never imagined possible.

In short, we will level the playing field between the financial elites and us.

I know some readers will want to know what is bitcoin? It's a new form of currency- like the dollar. It is the digital equivalent to cash.

A third source that we must look to for strong leadership is from the moderates of the white South. It is unfortunate that at this time the leadership of the white South stems from the close-minded reactionaries. These persons gain prominence and power by the dissemination of false ideas and by deliberately appealing to the deepest hate responses within the human mind. It is my firm belief that this close-minded, reactionary, recalcitrant group constitutes a numerical minority. There are in the white South more open-minded moderates than appears on the surface. These persons are silent today because of fear of social, political and economic reprisals. God grant that the white moderates of the South will rise up courageously, without fear, and take up the leadership in this tense period of transition.

I cannot close without stressing the urgent

need for strong, courageous and intelligent leadership from the Negro community. We need a leadership that is 1957 calm and yet positive. This is no day for the rabble-rouser, whether he be Negro or white. (*All right*) We must realize that we are grappling with the most weighty social problem of this nation, and in grappling with such a complex problem there is no place for misguided emotionalism. (*All right, that's right*) We must work passionately and unrelentingly for the goal of freedom, but we must be sure that our hands are clean in the struggle. We must never struggle with falsehood, hate, or malice. We must never become bitter. I know how we feel sometime. There is the danger that those of us who have been forced so long to stand amid the tragic midnight of oppression—those of us who have been trampled over, those of us who have been kicked about—there

But it doesn't have to go through a bank to exchange hands.

Bitcoin will provide Rich Pride with the freedom it needs to run on its own, but still gives us the opportunity to buy products from any other country.

For more information on bitcoin, google "Bitcoin" and you can find everything you need to know.

By using bitcoin, we will be able to control our own capital, which we must do in order to get ahead.

Bitcoin will change how we live as a people.

If you go into the real world you won't miss seeing that the poor are poor not because they are untrained or illiterate, but because they can't retain the return on their labor.

They have no control over Capital, and it's the ability to

control Capital that gives people the power to rise above poverty.

When we come together, we'll be able to control Capital and help our people rise above poverty.

Rich Pride will change the world. We have the potential to change the lives of people who need help getting ahead.

Bitcoin is our road to freedom. But even with bitcoin there is still a long road to travel; there is no easy walk to freedom anywhere.

It will allow us to try to relieve some of the poverty that ravagely throws the heart of the black community, throughout this country.

I don't know how many times, but I have to say it's up to "us" to change our way of living.

It's important for us to invest our money into our community.

is the danger that we will become bitter. But if we will become bitter and indulge in hate campaigns, the old, the new order which is emerging will be nothing but a duplication of the old order. (*Yeah, That's all right*)

We must meet hate with love. (*Yeah*) We must meet physical force with soul force. There is still a voice crying out through the vista of time, saying: "Love your enemies (*Yeah*), bless them that curse you (*Yes*), pray for them that despitefully use you."6(*That's right, All right*) Then, and only then, can you matriculate into the university of eternal life. That same voice cries out in terms lifted to cosmic proportions: "He who lives by the sword will perish by the sword."7(*Yeah, Lord*) And history is replete with the bleached bones of nations (*Yeah*) that failed to follow this command. (*All right*) We must follow nonviolence and love. (*Yes, Lord*)

Now, I'm not talking about a sentimental, shallow kind of love. (*Go ahead*) I'm not talking about eros, which is a sort of aesthetic, romantic love. I'm not even talking about philia, which is a sort of intimate affection between personal friends. But I'm talking about agape. (*Yes sir*) I'm talking about the love of God in the hearts of men. (*Yes*) I'm talking about a type of love which will cause you to love the person who does the evil deed while hating the deed that the person does. (*Go ahead*) We've got to love. (*Oh yes*)

There is another warning signal. We talk a great deal about our rights, and rightly so. We proudly proclaim that three-fourths of the peoples of the world are colored. We have the privilege of noticing in our generation the great drama of freedom and independence as it unfolds in Asia and Africa. All of these

Rich Pride will have its own form of government, we want a black state.

We want to inspire our people from conquered and servile community of yes man to militant and uncompromising band of comrades in arms. We want black privilege with political institutions, all black reserves, and tribal leaders.

On our land we want our own police, those who are there to understand the people and want to protect them.

We will call our land "The city of gold," and our police man will be a body of gentleman with clean hands.

We were not giving our 4o acres and a mule, so let's buy it ourselves.

We will create our own flag, national anthem, legislature, and constitutions.

Our members will fly the flag on their land and take pride, and what we built.

Being a member of the pride is something to brag about. It means you stand for something.

Any member that don't take pride in what we stand for will no longer be a part of the movement.

All members should disown any unloyal members, and they should be viewed as a trader.

Rich Pride flag will be black and white. The armed forces are used when all else has failed, when all channels of communication have been burned.

Our armed forces will protect our people on our land. It isn't our goal to start an uprising in America. But it is our goal to protect the people in our tribe.

things are in line with the unfolding work of Providence. But we must be sure that we accept them in the right spirit. We must not seek to use our emerging freedom and our growing power to do the same thing to the white minority that has been done to us for so many centuries. (*Yes*) Our aim must never be to defeat or humiliate the white man. We must not become victimized with a philosophy of black supremacy. God is not interested merely in freeing black men and brown men and yellow men, but God is interested in freeing the whole human race. (*Yes, All right*) We must work with determination to create a society (*Yes*), not where black men are superior and other men are inferior and vice versa, but a society in which all men will live together as brothers (*Yes*) and respect the dignity and worth of human personality. (*Yes*)

We must also avoid the temptation of being

victimized with a psychology of victors. We have won marvelous victories. Through the work of the NAACP, we have been able to do some of the most amazing things of this generation. And I come this afternoon with nothing, nothing but praise for this great organization, the work that it has already done and the work that it will do in the future. And although they're outlawed in Alabama and other states, the fact still remains that this organization has done more to achieve civil rights for Negroes than any other organization we can point to. (*Yeah, Amen*) Certainly, this is fine.

But we must not, however, remain satisfied with a court victory over our white brothers. We must respond to every decision with an understanding of those who have opposed us and with an appreciation of the difficult adjustments that the court orders

CHAPTER 5

"*A integrated cup of coffee isn't sufficient pay for four hundred years of slave labor.*"
—Malcom X.

Yesterday I was watching T.V and a police officer pulled over a white woman. She told the officer she was scared to reach for her phone on her lap, because of all the videos she'd seen on the internet of police killing people.

The officer responded by saying "They only kill Black people."

I was so upset that I almost cried. Just the thought of them intentionally killing our people like animals made my blood hot and my blood pressure rise.

After watching the news, I started working on this book. I wanted to get it done and start building our team.

I know if we stand alone they will continue getting away with killing us.

It really hurts my heart when I see the young ones acting like they don't care.

It's a shame no one cares until it's their love ones laying in the streets pumped with bullets from the people who took an oath to protect and serve.

Nobody cares until its them being racially profiled. And that's got to stop for change to come.

If we don't stand up and say, "no more," it will continue.

No more letting officers get away with murder, no more stopping black men because of the way we dress, or because they have dread locks in their hair.

pose for them. We must act in such a way as to make possible a coming together of white people and colored people on the basis of a real harmony of interest and understanding. We must seek an integration based on mutual respect.

I conclude by saying that each of us must keep faith in the future. Let us not despair. Let us realize that as we struggle for justice and freedom, we have cosmic companionship. This is the long faith of the Hebraic-Christian tradition: that God is not some Aristotelian "unmoved mover" who merely contemplates upon Himself. He is not merely a self-knowing God, but an other-loving God (*Yeah*) forever working through history for the establishment of His kingdom.

And those of us who call the name of Jesus Christ find something of an event in our Christian faith that tells us this. There is something in our faith that says to us, "Never despair; never give up; never feel that the cause of righteousness and justice is doomed." There is something in our Christian faith, at the center of it, which says to us that Good Friday may occupy the throne for a day, but ultimately it must give way to the triumphant beat of the drums of Easter.

(*That's right*) There is something in our faith that says evil may so shape events that Caesar will occupy the palace and Christ the cross (*That's right*), but one day that same Christ will rise up and split history into A.D. and B.C. (*Yes*), so that even the name, the life of Caesar must be dated by his name. (*Yes*) There is something in this universe (*Yes, Yes*) which justifies Carlyle in saying: "No lie can live forever." (*All right*) There is something in this universe which justifies William Cullen Bryant in saying: "Truth crushed to earth will rise again."

How could we call this the land of the free when not all people are treated the same?

I'm a believer that you get what you think you deserve. If we want small shit that's what we'll get.

We must dream big, we need plans that are over the top. Those ones that will take in abundance of hard work but are not impossible.

I feel anything is possible for us in today's society, and we need to remember that.

Black people are not all poor like most were a hundred years ago.

There are African Americans worth hundreds of millions of dollars. Our dreams are not just illusions they are attainable.

We plan to take things to the next level.

We understand we might have to pass through the valley of shadow of death again and again, before we reach the mountain of our desires.

But we do plan on reaching that mountain top. We plan on changing the future of blacks. But to do this we need "You" to join and be willing to fight for the things people will try saying we don't deserve.

Starting a black tribe in America won't be easy at all, but the things that are worth have never come easy. Build a potential following will be extraordinary hard. Because people have been told that taking pride in their race makes them racist.

But that's not the major problem we'll face. The biggest problem is that most of our young blacks believe it's not cool to participate in politics. They don't

(*Yes, All right*) There is something in this universe (*Watch yourself*) which justifies James Russell Lowell in saying:

Truth forever on the scaffold,

Wrong forever on the throne. (*Oh yeah*)

Yet that scaffold sways the future,

And behind the dim unknown

Stands God (*All right*), within the shadow,

Keeping watch above His own.8 (*Yeah, Yes*)

Go out with that faith today. (*All right, Yes*) Go back to your homes in the Southland to that faith, with that faith today. Go back to Philadelphia, to New York, to 1957 Detroit and Chicago with that faith today (*That's right*), that the universe is on our side in the struggle. (*Sure is, Yes*) Stand up for justice. (*Yes*) Sometimes it gets hard, but it is always difficult to get out of Egypt, for the Red Sea always stands before you with discouraging dimensions. (*Yes*) And even after you've crossed the Red Sea, you have to move through a wilderness with prodigious hilltops of evil (*Yes*) and gigantic mountains of opposition. (*Yes*) But I say to you this afternoon: Keep moving. (*Go on ahead*) Let nothing slow you up. (*Go on ahead*) Move on with dignity and honor and respectability. (*Yes*)

I realize that it will cause restless nights sometime. It might cause losing a job; it will cause suffering and sacrifice. (*That's right*) It might even cause physical death for some. But if physical death is the price that some must pay (*Yes sir*) to free their children from a permanent life of psychological death (*Yes sir*), then nothing can be more Christian. (*Yes sir*) Keep going today. (*Yes sir*) Keep moving amid every obstacle. (*Yes sir*) Keep moving amid every mountain of opposition. (*Yes sir, Yeah*) If you will do

believe in the system or the US government willingness to allow them to participate and making a difference.

Most young blacks believe that a lot of black based political movements are corrupt. Because of some past movements that weren't successful, they can't wrap their head around some things that might work.

But Rich Pride is the situation to these problems. Our members won't have to worry about where their money is going.

Because we believe what our members do with their money is their business, but what we do with their money is everyone's business.

This kind of transparency will open a whole new industry, it is not only with Rich Pride but with other groups as well. Anybody that wants to use our people and hold our commodities on a way we can't check in on them will be exposed. It will make it hard on these people to do any kind of corrupt business.

We understand that our members will want to know (A) the money they are putting in is safe, and (B) they want transparency…

Our investors will be able to see what's going on. Every member will know what's going on. And we'll provide transparency. And we will ease their trust issues with love and transparency. By showing we can prosper together without hating on one another, without pulling each other down, to succeed on our own.

All we ask of our members is not to join Rich Pride for themselves, join for a chance to help own the future, for a chance to build something our kids will be proud to be a part of.

that with dignity (*Say it*), when the history books are written in the future, the historians will have to look back and say, "There lived a great people. (*Yes sir, Yes*) A people with 'fleecy locks and black complexion,' but a people who injected new meaning into the veins of civilization (*Yes*); a people which stood up with dignity and honor and saved Western civilization in her darkest hour (*Yes*); a people that gave new integrity and a new dimension of love to our civilization."9(*Yeah, Look out*) When that happens, "the morning stars will sing together (*Yes sir*), and the sons of God will shout for joy."10(*Yes sir, All right*) [*applause*] (*Yes, That's wonderful, All right*)

At. MLKJP-GAMK.

This is still a problem today, but the ballot is not being taking away from all African Americans, just the 451,100 sentenced prisoners. The U.S imprison more residents then any other nation, both in term of total prisoners and its incarcerated rate.

SPEECH TO THE AFRICAN SUMMIT CONFERENCE (AUGUST 21, 1964) MALCOM X

The Organization of Afro-American Unity has sent me to attend this historic African Summit Conference as an observer to represent the interests of 22 million African-Americans whose human rights are being violated daily by the racism of American imperialists.

The Organization of Afro-American Unity has been formed by a cross section of America's African-American community, and is patterned after the letter and spirit of the Organization of African Unity.

Just as the Organization of African Unity has called upon all African leaders to submerge their differences and unite on common objectives for the common good of all

We all must see the vision to make it come true. We must dream so far ahead that when the future comes, we'll be right there with nations that started hundreds of years before us.

We're playing catch up but were up for the challenge. We're more than ready to hold the weight of the world on our shoulders.

The day has come and we're here ready to deliver our people to the promise land of our own, one that we won't have to fight for everything.

CHAPTER 6

"You never hear of black people in this country talking or speaking or thinking in terms of connecting themselves with their own kind back home."
—Malcom X.

Have you ever laid back and just thought about the state of the black race? The black on black crime, drug dealing, and so many black men get sentenced to decades in prison? All the kids growing up without fathers, the gangs, and how some have misled the young brothers.

How our young soldiers kill each other in the name of colors but won't stand up and protect each other against cops who maltreat them.

Africans, in America the Organization of Afro-American Unity has called upon Afro-American leaders to submerge their differences and find areas of agreement wherein we can work in unity for the good of the entire 22 million African Americans.

Since the 22 million of us were originally Africans, who are now in America, not by choice but only by a cruel accident in our history, we strongly believe that African problems are our problems and our problems are African problems.

We also believe that as heads of the independent African states you are the shepherds of all African peoples everywhere, whether they are still at home here on the mother continent or have been scattered abroad.

Some African leaders at this conference have implied that they have enough problems here on the mother continent without adding the Afro-American problem.

With all due respect to your esteemed positions, I must remind all of you that the Good Shepherd will leave ninety-nine sheep who are safe at home to go to the aid of the one who is lost and has fallen into the clutches of the imperialist wolf.

We in America are your long-lost brothers and sisters, and I am here only to remind you that our problems are your problems. As the African-Americans "awaken" today, we find ourselves in a strange land that has rejected us, and, like the prodigal son, we are turning to our elder brothers for help. We pray our pleas will not fall upon deaf ears.

We were taken forcibly in chains from this mother continent and have now spent over three hundred years in America, suffering the most inhuman forms of physical and psychological tortures imaginable.

Have you ever had sleepless nights after watching a black male get gunned down on T.V., only to see the officer walk free months later?

If you haven't, then you won't understand what motivates me. You won't understand the pain inside my body, the vision inside my head, the goals I have, and the mission I'm on.

If you haven't had one of these moments, the pride is more than likely not for you.

We want people with passion so deep that when they think about how bright our future will be they can't sleep, members who read this book will come up with ideas that make this vision better.

I'm writing this book to put my ideas on paper. So that we have a ledger to begin the process of building our pride and make the movement more than just a thought.

As I'm writing this I'm having thoughts it won't work. I believe if we get big the government will do whatever possible to sabotage the movement, like they've done in the past.

But some part of me wants to believe we live for a better time. So, I push forward with the mission.

I would fear for my life if it wasn't for social media and smart phones to tape everything that's done.

Things have change so much that governments must worry about whistle blower. So, I don't think there will be any attempt on my life.

I plan to lead this mission, even if I must die for what I believe in, because I understand what we're

During the past ten years the entire world has witnessed our men, women, and children being attacked and bitten by vicious police dogs, brutally beaten by police clubs, and washed down the sewers by high- pressure water hoses that would rip the clothes from our bodies and the flesh from our limbs.

And all of these inhuman atrocities have been inflicted upon us by the American governmental authorities, the police themselves, for no reason other than that we seek the recognition and respect granted other human beings in America.

The American Government is either unable or unwilling to protect the lives and property of your 22 million African-American brothers and sisters. We stand defenseless, at the mercy of American racists who murder us at will for no reason other than we are black and of African descent.

Last week an unarmed African-American educator was murdered in cold blood in Georgia; a few days before that three civil rights workers disappeared completely, perhaps murdered also, only because they were teaching our people in Mississippi how to vote and how to secure their political rights.

Our problems are your problems. We have lived for over three hundred years in that American den of racist wolves in constant fear of losing life and limb. Recently, three students from Kenya were mistaken for American Negroes and were brutally beaten by the New York police. Shortly after that two diplomats from Uganda were also beaten by the New York City police, who mistook them for American Negroes.

If Africans are brutally beaten while only visiting in America, imagine the physical and psychological suffering received by your brothers and sisters who have lived

trying to build is bigger than my life, it's bigger than that of any individual.

I know some people are going to read this and think that I'm crazy for thinking someone would kill me over my thoughts, and dreams of a better future for the black race. But think of what happened to Malcom X, Martin Luther King, and so many other revolutionists. For some reason the government don't want us to come together. It might have something to do with the fact that everything we do we exceed expectation, once we have time to learn from our mistakes and try again. We get better each time.

There's no doubt in my mind a hundred years from now our economy will stand toe to toe with the best this world has to offer. Our land will bring in tourist for all over the world.

Our armed forces will be able to protect us from any nation.

I have no problem saying things, because I believe them with all my heart. I know there are people out there ready to stand up and hold some of the load of our prosperity.

We will own companies. We will raise above just workers. We want to build an economy that will not only thrive but do so well that all our members will be rich.

I want what we all deserve, and I want to have the things our ancestors deserved but never got. I want to stand tall one day and be proud of what "We" accomplished.

I want to see black kids grow up and protect each other instead of laying each other down. I want to see them 30 clips used to watch over our people instead

there for over three hundred years.

Our problem is your problem. No matter how much independence Africans get here on the mother continent, unless you wear your national dress at all time when you visit America, you may be mistaken for one of us and suffer the same psychological and physical mutilation that is an everyday occurrence in our lives.

Your problems will never be fully solved until and unless ours are solved. You will never be fully respected until and unless we are also respected. You will never be recognized as free human beings until and unless we are also recognized and treated as human beings.

Our problem is your problem. It is not a Negro problem, nor an American problem. This is a world problem, a problem for humanity. It is not a problem of civil rights, it is a problem of human rights.

We pray that our African brothers have not freed themselves of European colonialism only to be overcome and held in check now by American dollarism. Don't let American racism be "legalized" by American dollarism.

America is worse than South Africa, because not only is America racist, but she is also deceitful and hypocritical. South Africa preaches segregation and practices segregation. She, at least, practices what she preaches. America preaches integration and practices segregation. She preaches one thing while deceitfully practicing another. South Africa is like a vicious wolf, openly hostile toward black humanity. But America is cunning like a fox, friendly and smiling, but even more vicious and deadly than the wolf.

The wolf and the fox are both enemies of humanity, both are canine, both humiliate

of standing over them pumping them full of bullets.

I want to see it all, but I understand I might not live to see my dreams come true. I may not watch our land get built, but I'm okay with that if my kids and all members kids could see a strong black empire. I'm cool with it if the black race isn't one of the poorest people on earth. Money is power, and influence; we want to be able to influence the world.

CHAPTER 7

"Truth will stand us on own feet. Truth will make us walk for ourselves instead of leaning on others who mean our people no good. Truth not only shows us who our real enemy is, truth also gives us the strength and the know-how to separate ourselves from that enemy."
—**Malcom X.**

Education is very important, it's the future of Rich Pride and the future of the world.

We need to educate our younger members, so they will be prepared to take the dream to places we never imagined.

So, they know how much what we're doing means to our people. Our schools will compete with and mutilate their victims. Both have the same objectives, but differ only in methods.

If South Africa is guilty of violating the human rights of Africans here on the mother continent, then America is guilty of worse violations of the 22 million Africans on the American continent. And if South African racism is not a domestic issue, then American racism also is not a domestic issue. We beseech independent African states to help us bring our problem before the United Nations, on the grounds that the United States Government is morally incapable of protecting the lives and the property of 22 million African-Americans. And on the grounds that our deteriorating plight is definitely becoming a threat to world peace.

Out of frustration and hopelessness our young people have reached the point of no return. We no longer endorse patience and turning the other cheek. We assert the right of self-defense by whatever means necessary, and reserve the right of maximum retaliation against our racist oppressors, no matter what the odds against us are.

We are well aware that our future efforts to defend ourselves by retaliating—by meeting violence with violence, eye for eye and tooth for tooth—could create the type of racial conflict in America that could easily escalate into a violent, worldwide, bloody race war. In the interests of world peace and security, we beseech the heads of the independent African states to recommend an immediate investigation into our problem by the United Nations Commission on Human Rights.

One last word, my beloved brothers at this African Summit: "No one knows the master better than his servant." We have been servants in America for over three hundred years. We have a thorough inside

schools around the world to be the best academically.

Our people can lead in building cars, phones, and doing everything that's meaningful. Our teachers will get paid more than any other job, because they are the ones shaping our future leaders.

One thing I don't understand about the U.S government is why lawyers and judges get paid more than teachers. To me, that makes no sense whatsoever.

A hundred years from now, our kids will make the discovery that will change the world.

It's my dream to see kids go to school all year around, but I know this won't make them happy. But if we're going to make up for years of slavery and the years we spent with not so much meaningful progress at all, we're going to need to work harder than ever before.

If our kids get use to challenging work, it will be easier for them to maintain this type of mindset. It would be easier to do what is necessary to obtain our future goals. Some people will think these are the goals of only a few individuals, but that's not true, these should be the goals of the Black race. Even if some believe it shouldn't be.

A hundred years from now Rich Pride will be viewed as the saviors of our race. They will write history books about the people that took part in this movement.

They will call them revolutionaries. People will look back at where the future of the black race was headed, and created us for changing the path of destruction, and where we were headed for. Our member will walk on our land and feel a sense of joy to call it home.

knowledge of this man who calls himself "Uncle Sam." Therefore, you must heed our warning. Don't escape from European colonialism only to become even more enslaved by deceitful,"friendly" American dollarism. May Allah's blessings of good health and wisdom be upon you all

There still isn't a strong bond between Africans, and African Americans today, something we plan to fix.

"A DECLARATION OF INDEPENDENCE" MALCOM X

Because 1964 threatens to be a very explosive year on the racial front, and because I myself intend to be very active in every phase of the American Negro struggle for human rights, I have called this press conference this morning in order to clarify my own position in the struggle—especially in regard to politics and nonviolence.

I am and always will be a Muslim. My religion

is Islam. I still believe that Mr. Muhammad's analysis of the problem is the most realistic, and that his solution is the best one. This means that I too believe the best solution is complete separation, with our people going back home, to our own African homeland.

But separation back to Africa is still a long-range program, and while it is yet to materialize, 22 million of our people who are still here in America need better food, clothing, housing, education and jobs right now. Mr. Muhammad's program does point us back homeward, but it also contains within it what we could and should be doing to help solve many of our own problems while we are still here.

Internal differences within the Nation of Islam forced me out of it. I did not leave of my own free will. But now that it has happened, I intend to make the most of it. Now that I have more independence of

There will be a block party every year to celebrate our achievements. People of all races will come together and party like its New Year's Eve.

Every race would want to participate, because they will know we helped make the world a safer place. A place where kids don't get shot walking home from school. A place where they could sit and play in their neighborhood without worrying about shot's being fired.

We will create a world where most of blacks won't live in the ghetto. The native Americans were able to build an empire within the U.S.A, so why can't we? We have no reason to fail, if we are together. We are strong but were stronger together.

There is truly strength in number.

CHAPTER 8

"Jesus himself prophesied: You shall know the truth and it shall make you free. Beloved brothers and sisters Jesus never said that Abraham Lincoln would make us free. He never said that congress would make us free. He never said that senate or Supreme Court or John Kinnedy would make us free. Jesus two thousand years ago looked down the wheel of time and saw your and my plight and he knew the tricky high court, sleep, and tricky promises of the hypocritical politicians on civil right legislation would only be designed to advance you and me from ancient slavery to modern slavery."

—**Malcom X**

It is said in democracy that people get to choose their

action, I intend to use a more flexible approach toward working with others to get a solution to this problem.

I do not pretend to be a divine man, but I do believe in divine guidance, divine power, and in the fulfillment of divine prophecy. I am not educated, nor am I an expert in any particular field—but I am sincere, and my sincerity is my credential.

I'm not out to fight other Negro leaders or organizations. We must find a common approach, a common solution, to a common problem. As of this minute, I've forgotten everything bad that the other leaders have said about me, and I pray they can also forget the many bad things I've said about them.

The problem facing our people here in America is bigger than all other personal or organizational differences. Therefore, as leaders, we must stop worrying about the threat that we seem to think we pose to each other's personal prestige, and concentrate our united efforts toward solving the unending hurt that is being done daily to our people here in America.

I am going to organize and head a new mosque in New York City, known as the Muslim Mosque Incorporated. This gives us a religious base, and the spiritual force necessary to rid our people of the vices that destroy the moral fiber of our community.

Our political philosophy will be black nationalism. Our economic and social philosophy will be black nationalism. Our cultural emphasis will be black nationalism.

Many of our people aren't religiously inclined, so the Muslim Mosque Incorporated, will be organized in such manner to provide for the active participation of all Negroes in our political, economic, and social programs, despite

government, but that isn't completely true. Especially in democratic, republicans like the U.S.A., what they really mean is that we get to choose aspects of our government. A person can't vote to turn their government into the French government, or whatever government they prefer. They can vote on things, but they are usually stuck with the one they have.

But Rich Pride will create a mechanism when it is installed, we'll be creating a workable direct democracy. Arguable for the first time, if someone was injured on the job, and must stop working. The members could decide if they deserve their retirement early, and how that retirement would be handled.

Citizens will be able to vote how much money will be spent on schools, road, police, and everything else in a direct way, right on their cell phones or computers or whatever strange technology they are using in the future.

Rich Pride future is bright, because people at the bottom have the power of nothing to lose.

We have so many complex proposals including our own banks, which will function both as a place to store cryptocurrencies, and to go to for loans.

The bank will look at a person's credit within the Pride, and their proof of income, and other aspects before deciding to finance a loan. A person's credit with the U.S government won't matter if they are a member of Rich Pride.

But if the borrower doesn't pay back the loan they will be black listed. The profits raised from these loans will be used to give interest to the participants

their religious or non-religious beliefs.

The political philosophy of black nationalism means: we must control the politics and the politicians of our community. They must no longer take orders from outside forces. We will organize, and sweep out of office all Negro politicians who are puppets for the outside forces.

Our accent will be upon youth: we need new ideas, new methods, new approaches. We will call upon young students of political science throughout the nation to help us. We will encourage these young students to launch their own independent study, and then give us their analysis and their suggestions. We are completely disenchanted with the old, adult, established politicians. We want to see some new faces— more militant faces.

Concerning the 1964 elections: we will keep our plans on this a secret until a later date—but we don't intend for our people to be the victims of a political sellout again in 1964.

The Muslim Mosque Incorporated, will remain wide open for ideas and financial aid from all quarters. Whites can help us, but they can't join us. There can be no black-white unity until there is first some black unity. There can be no workers' solidarity until there is first some racial solidarity. We cannot think of uniting with others, until after we have first united among ourselves. We cannot think of being acceptable to others until we have first proven acceptable to ourselves. One can't unite bananas with scattered leaves.

Concerning nonviolence: it is criminal to teach a man not to defend himself when he is the constant victim of brutal attacks. It is legal and lawful to own a shotgun or a rifle. We believe in obeying the law.

who put their money into this automated bank.

The first members will benefit tremendously. They will have the opportunity of being first to invest in big ideas.

I want to set an example for my race. I don't want to use them as a source of power.

On land owned by Rich Pride all clubs, hotels, and gas stations will be own by Rich Pride. The money from these organizations will be used to fund our tribe.

I can't stress this enough, that I know. We face an uphill battle building an organization meant to build up the black race in a county riddled with inform, where blacks could arbitrarily be stopped and searched at any moment, will be monumentally difficult.

I know they will give us a tough time, but it won't stop us. For hundreds of years they have told us, we couldn't do this or that, but once giving the chance, we exceed expectations.

Rich Pride is just an idea until we find people who believe in the movement. It is an interesting idea, but there are many steps between where we are now and the potential future.

This book is a recruiting tool not policy. This project might bring a form of black democracy to the people, even if it's not in the form of our own government.

Rich Pride wants to become the brain trust, and the power station for Black Nationalism.

In areas where our people are the constant victims of brutality, and the government seems unable or unwilling to protect them, we should form rifle clubs that can be used to defend our lives and our property in times of emergency, such as happened last year in Birmingham; Plaquemine, Louisiana; Cambridge, Maryland; and Danville, Virginia. When our people are being bitten by dogs, they are within their rights to kill those dogs. We should be peaceful, law-abiding—but the time has come for the American Negro to fight back in self-defense whenever and wherever he is being unjustly and unlawfully attacked.

If the government thinks I am wrong for saying this, then let the government start doing its job.

Although we do not agree with Malcom X views on race, we agree that it's up to black man to change the life of poverty that so many of us face today.

CHAPTER 9

"Only a blind man will walk into the open embrace of his enemy."
—**Malcom X.**

We call on all black man in prison to join Rich Pride. We want to give you all the right to vote and make a different back. We want you all to be able to participate in something great again.

We believe the justice system is a prison for black man. Most of the laws have been made to keep us down. This is known around the world, but law makers won't change these laws.

Rich Pride doesn't want to blame all the black's problems with the justice system on the government, because we are the ones breaking these laws, so some of these responsibilities belong to us. But the way the black man is sentenced is the difference between the races. They are being given more time than their white counterparts.

We call on all reformed inmates to think about the times you were racially profiled. Think about all the years of not belonging in feeling maltreated. Once you're done, join Rich Pride, to make sure your kids won't go through this.

Help us build a future like we only can dream of.

We know there are great minds behind bars who will be able to add to our system, help our tribe, and we call on them for assistants.

But only if they believe in our goals and want to be a part of the solution not the problem.

material prosperity. One hundred years later, the Negro is still languished in the corners of American society and finds himself an exile in his own land. And so we've come here today to dramatize a shameful condition.

In a sense we've come to our nation's capital to cash a check. When the architects of our republic wrote the magnificent words of the Constitution and the **DECLARATION OF INDEPENDENCE**, they were signing a promissory note to which every American was to fall heir. This note was a promise that all men, yes, black men as well as white men, would be guaranteed the "unalienable Rights" of "Life, Liberty and the pursuit of Happiness." It is obvious today that America has defaulted on this promissory note, insofar as her citizens of color are concerned. Instead of honoring this sacred obligation, America has given the Negro people a bad check, a check which has come back marked "insufficient funds."

But we refuse to believe that the bank of justice is bankrupt. We refuse to believe that there are insufficient funds in the great vaults of opportunity of this nation. And so, we've come to cash this check, a check that will give us upon demand the riches of freedom and the security of justice.

We have also come to this hallowed spot to remind America of the fierce urgency of Now. This is no time to engage in the luxury of cooling off or to take the tranquilizing drug of gradualism. Now is the time to make real the promises of democracy. Now is the time to rise from the dark and desolate valley of segregation to the sunlit path of racial justice. Now is the time to lift our nation from the quicksands of racial injustice to the solid rock of brotherhood. Now is the time to make justice a reality for all of God's children.

We don't want to tell our members how to live, and we never will, but we won't allow insubordination.

Our flag should be on every member's Facebook page as their cover photo not the profile photo. Being a member of Rich Pride should be an honor and should not, and no way be hidden.

We call on all prisoners who want to use their time to strengthen up their mind. Prisoners who have learned about the government system used to keep us down.

We're looking for prisoners who see the vision and the opportunity that are ahead of us.

We want the man and woman, who are strong enough to fight for something, that's bigger than them.

We're not looking for individuals filled with greed, because greed has brought down some of the strongest empires.

What we're building will last hundreds of years.

At this point in most prisoners' life, the government has written them off as failures, but Rich Pride is looking to make them revolutionaries. To all prisoners that read this book, I say, it's not the end of the road, you still have a chance to participate in something meaningful, you still can make an impact on the future. You could help change the future for your kids.

We want prisoners to join, because not only have they felt the struggle of being in prison but have lived through the oppression of blacks by the government.

We believe they will be motivated and there's nothing like the motivation of an oppressed man.

It would be fatal for the nation to overlook the urgency of the moment. This sweltering summer of the Negro's legitimate discontent will not pass until there is an invigorating autumn of freedom and equality. Nineteen sixty-three is not an end, but a beginning. And those who hope that the Negro needed to blow off steam and will now be content will have a rude awakening if the nation returns to business as usual. And there will be neither rest nor tranquility in America until the Negro is granted his citizenship rights. The whirlwinds of revolt will continue to shake the foundations of our nation until the bright day of justice emerges.

But there is something that I must say to my people, who stand on the warm threshold which leads into the palace of justice: In the process of gaining our rightful place, we must not be guilty of wrongful deeds. Let us not seek to satisfy our thirst for freedom by drinking from the cup of bitterness and hatred. We must forever conduct our struggle on the high plane of dignity and discipline. We must not allow our creative protest to degenerate into physical violence. Again and again, we must rise to the majestic heights of meeting physical force with soul force.

The marvelous new militancy which has engulfed the Negro community must not lead us to a distrust of all white people, for many of our white brothers, as evidenced by their presence here today, have come to realize that their destiny is tied up with our destiny. And they have come to realize that their freedom is inextricably bound to our freedom.

We cannot walk alone.

And as we walk, we must make the pledge that we shall always march ahead.

We cannot turn back.

We want to turn this motivation into something they could be proud of. Something a hundred years from now their kids could be proud of as well. They will be able to say their parents helped build something that change their world.

Think about the future now! Think about where you are. What you want to be remembered for!!! What do you want your legacy to be?

Take the time to think about how you want the world to be, when you're gone. Most people don't think this far ahead. But Rich Pride is, were thinking so far ahead, to make plans that will last two or three life times. Our plans will affect the generation that comes after us.

We're thinking ahead to make up for the generation that came before us, because they stopped planning and started using drugs. We're planning and believing for the people who don't. We're dreaming for the people who are scared to think big.

We're calling on prisoners to open their eyes. We're calling on them to invest their time and their visions with us, because they have the time to dream big. They have the time to really think about what they "wish" they could have.

There are those who are asking the devotees of civil rights, "When will you be satisfied?" We can never be satisfied as long as the Negro is the victim of the unspeakable horrors of police brutality. We can never be satisfied as long as our bodies, heavy with the fatigue of travel, cannot gain lodging in the motels of the highways and the hotels of the cities. **We cannot be satisfied as long as the negro's basic mobility is from a smaller ghetto to a larger one. We can never be satisfied as long as our children are stripped of their self-hood and robbed of their dignity by signs stating: "For Whites Only."** We cannot be satisfied as long as a Negro in Mississippi cannot vote and a Negro in New York believes he has nothing for which to vote. No, no, we are not satisfied, and we will not be satisfied until «justice rolls down like waters, and righteousness like a mighty stream.»

CHAPTER 10

I am not unmindful that some of you have come here out of great trials and tribulations. Some of you have come fresh from narrow jail cells. And some of you have come from areas where your quest — quest for freedom left you battered by the storms of persecution and staggered by the winds of police brutality.

You have been the veterans of creative suffering. Continue to work with the faith that unearned suffering is redemptive. Go back to Mississippi, go back to Alabama, go back to South Carolina, go back to Georgia, go back to Louisiana, go back to the slums and ghettos of our northern cities, knowing that somehow this situation can and will be changed.

Let us not wallow in the valley of despair, I say to you today, my friends.

And so even though we face the difficulties of today and tomorrow, I still have a dream. It is a dream deeply rooted in the American dream.

"The poor so-called Negro, he doesn't control the NAACP, he can't control the urban league, he can't control his own schools, he can't control his own businesses in his own community. He can't control his own mind. He's lost and lost control of himself and gone astray."
—Malcom X

Rich Pride wants to create a tribe for blacks. But we will be committed to involving all races and political groups in our future campaign. We want a black state, but do not seek to segregate the blacks from the rest of the world. What we want is to build a black empire that caters for the development of our people.

We want to create a revitalized mass bass for black men, not just America but all over the world.

Rich Pride wants to learn from the past, and make sure no race ever looks down on our people again.

Back in slavery days the white men realized to make a content slave they must make a thoughtless one, one whose mental visions are darkened.

Once a slave was purchased, he had to be marked as property. We want to make sure our future looks bright, not dark.

We should own property not be it. Back in slavery days, whites refused to work with free colored workers. They feared that it would lead to less opportunities of employment for poor whites. They thought all workers of color should be killed before they took over the country.

I have a dream that one day this nation will rise up and live out the true meaning of its creed: "We hold these truths to be self-evident, that all men are created equal."

I have a dream that one day on the red hills of Georgia, the sons of former slaves and the sons of former slave owners will be able to sit down together at the table of brotherhood.

I have a dream that one day even the state of Mississippi, a state sweltering with the heat of injustice, sweltering with the heat of oppression, will be transformed into an oasis of freedom and justice.

I have a dream that my four little children will one day live in a nation where they will not be judged by the color of their skin but by the content of their character.

I have a *dream* today!

I have a dream that one day, down in Alabama, with its vicious racists, with its governor having his lips dripping with the words of "interposition" and "nullification" — one day right there in Alabama little black boys and black girls will be able to join hands with little white boys and white girls as sisters and brothers.

I have a ***dream*** today!

I have a dream that one day every valley shall be exalted, and every hill and mountain shall be made low, the rough places will be made plain, and the crooked places will be made straight; "and the glory of the Lord shall be revealed and all flesh shall see it together."[2]

This is our hope, and this is the faith that I go back to the South with.

With this faith, we will be able to hew out of the mountain of despair a stone of hope. With this faith, we will be able to transform the jangling discords of our nation into a beautiful symphony of brotherhood. With this faith, we will be able to work together, to pray together, to struggle

What we plan to do is stop the mindset of blacks whose only wish is to be workers. We want to inspire all blacks to become bosses.

We don't want to just get by, we want to ball. There is nothing that's impossible for us today; we are a free man, we could learn and go to school — something some blacks were killed for. There were no schools for slaves' children. They were taught with the help of a whip. They used to tell blacks that "god" made it for whites to be masters and for blacks to be slaves.

They thought it was unlawful, and unsafe to teach a "nigger" how to read. A "nigger" should know nothing but how to obey his master. But times have changed, and we have knowledge on our side, and we have made the pathway from slavery to a free man.

It's time we take the next step and begin to own the world, instead of being workers. Rich Pride knows one day the black race will have influence over the world.

Our business will be successful, they won't be able to ignore us. We are just beginning, and at this stage, we still need to mobilize and start fundraising our movement.

We plan to host celebrations and party as fundraising opportunity to finance the beginning of our tribe. I believe this alone will be enough to get us started, and from there the sky is the limit.

We will transform blacks from being the poorest in America to be the greatest empire this world has ever seen. We understand this won't happen overnight. And it might take centuries.

But if it's up to Rich Pride, it will happen. We know, we can create together, to go to jail together, to stand up for freedom together, knowing that we will be free one day.

And this will be the day — this will be the day when all of God's children will be able to sing with new meaning:

My country 'tis of thee, sweet land of liberty, of thee I sing. Land where my fathers died, land of the Pilgrim's pride,   From every mountainside, let freedom ring!

And if America is to be a great nation, this must become true.

And so let freedom ring from the prodigious hilltops of New Hampshire.

Let freedom ring from the mighty mountains of New York.

Let freedom ring from the heightening Alleghenies of Pennsylvania.

Let freedom ring from the snow-capped Rockies of Colorado.

Let freedom ring from the curvaceous slopes of California.

But not only that:

Let freedom ring from Stone Mountain of Georgia.

Let freedom ring from Lookout Mountain of Tennessee.

Let freedom ring from every hill and molehill of Mississippi.

From every mountainside, let freedom ring.

I have a *dream* today!

I have a dream that one day every valley shall be exalted, and every hill and mountain shall be made low, the rough places will be made plain, and the crooked places will be made straight; "and the glory of the Lord shall be revealed and all flesh shall see it together."[2]

This is our hope, and this is the faith that I go back to the South with.

With this faith, we will be able to hew out of the mountain of despair a stone of hope. With this faith, we will be able to transform the jangling discords of our nation into a beautiful symphony of a movement, where people will be proud of our people.

We won't be looked down on by any other race. We will invest in each other, and believe the next black person is watching our backs instead of waiting to rob or kill us.

Our moment is now, and we must believe and participate instead of sitting on our ass and watching. We have a real problem with waiting and hoping somebody else will make change when we all need to be a part of change.

All Rich Pride wants is to build a culture that will change the way blacks are perceived and change the life of poverty most blacks face every day. We see that the world hasn't been great to us. We have been held down on so many levels, and it will continue until we say enough.

We won't stand back and watch future generations be maltreated and oppressed like the generations that came before them.

Blacks need to invest in our people's future. We need to take all the pain from being racially profiled, from being followed around stores like we're about to take something that doesn't belong to us and put that pain and tears into this movement. Become a member of Rich Pride as soon as possible.

brotherhood. With this faith, we will be able to work together, to pray together, to struggle together, to go to jail together, to stand up for freedom together, knowing that we will be free one day.

And this will be the day — this will be the day when all of God's children will be able to sing with new meaning:

My country 'tis of thee, sweet land of liberty, of thee I sing. Land where my fathers died, land of the Pilgrim's pride,   From every mountainside, let freedom ring!

And if America is to be a great nation, this must become true.

And so let freedom ring from the prodigious hilltops of New Hampshire.

Let freedom ring from the mighty mountains of New York.

Let freedom ring from the heightening Alleghenies of Pennsylvania.

Let freedom ring from the snow-capped Rockies of Colorado.

Let freedom ring from the curvaceous slopes of California.

But not only that:

Let freedom ring from Stone Mountain of Georgia. Let freedom ring from Lookout Mountain of Tennessee.

Let freedom ring from every hill and molehill of Mississippi.

From every mountainside, let freedom ring.

And when this happens, and when we allow freedom ring, when we let it ring from every village and every hamlet, from every state and every city, we will be able to speed up that day when *all* of God's children, black men and white men, Jews and Gentiles, Protestants and Catholics, will be able to join hands and sing in the words of the old Negro spiritual:

Free at last! Free at last!

Thank God Almighty, we are free at last!

CHAPTER 11

"God must destroy the world of slavery and evil in order to establish a world based upon freedom, justice, and equality."
—Malcom X

Becoming a member of Rich Pride won't be easy, but if that deter you and make you say, "fuck it" we don't want you any ways.

We are looking for people willing to fight. We want the people who are determined and want to change the world. There is no place in Rich Pride for the weak minded. There is no room for blacks who want to oppress their own people, by sitting on their ass doing nothing.

This is a movement of action, not some lazy asses. We want to see our members rich, that's why it's called Rich Pride.

It's time to build on fate and family. Let's have fate. We can solve any problem that comes our way. We don't need the government to step in and save our race.

We're building a family willing to do anything to help one another. A family that's willing to make sacrifices for our community. It will be a lot of work to change the path of our people. But I have fate that in the end we will win, at everything we do in this country. And one day it will lead to the independence of the black race, and to a black state.

There was a time when we couldn't dare pronounce these words, because we knew what would happen. Our people used to fight for their life's, for

MICHELLE OBAMA NEW HEMPSIRE POWERFUL SPEECH

My goodness! You guys are fired up!

Well, let me just say hello everyone. I am so thrilled to be here with you all today in New Hampshire. This is like home to me, and this day – thank you for a beautiful fall day. You just ordered this day up for me, didn't you? It's great to be here.

Let me start by thanking your fabulous governor, your next US senator, Maggie Hassan. I want to thank her for that lovely introduction. I also want to recognize your Congresswoman Annie McKlane Kuster, who's a dear, dear friend. Your soon-to-be congresswoman once again, Carol Shea Porter – all of whom have been just terrific friends to us. And your executive council and candidate for governor, Colin Van Ostern.

And, of course, thanks to all of you for taking the time to be here today.

Thanks so much. That's very sweet of you. I love you guys too. I can't believe it's just a few weeks before election day, as we come together to support the next president and vice-president of the United States, <u>Hillary Clinton</u> and Tim Kaine! And New Hampshire is going to be important, as always.

So I'm going to get a little serious here, because I think we can all agree that this has been a rough week in an already rough election. This week has been particularly interesting for me personally because it has been a week of profound contrast.

See, on Tuesday, at the White House, we celebrated the International Day of the Girl and Let Girls Learn, and it was a wonderful celebration. It was the last event that I'm going to be doing as first lady for Let Girls Learn. And I had the pleasure of spending

their safety, and to accomplish anything in this nation.

But now we must fight for blacks' honor, and it will one day lead to our independence.

Rich Pride accepts the task of walking us over these roads. We are the front line, all we ask of our people is to give us the possibility of moving forward with the struggle.

Money will be needed to establish ourselves. Our members need to realize the peril of our situation: we need to do what is necessary to get ahead.

What we are trying do isn't impossible. Israel was proclaimed only 69 years ago and look how far they have come. They believed and what was right for their people, and with time they made it happen.

Sometimes it seems that only a miracle can save our people, but we're not in need of a miracle, what we need is love from our people in hard work.

Our management and care will be entrusted to our members, for once our people will be in control. We are not threatened by the existence of any organization, we just want to uplift the black men.

We won't be pussyfooting or compromising. We know what we want, and that won't change. But we will hold discussions and listen to our members to hear their ideas, and solutions and answers to any of our problems.

Rich Pride will work with anybody who is genuinely interested in taking the problem of poverty in the black community head on.

hours talking to some of the most amazing young women you will ever meet, young girls here in the US and all around the world. And we talked about their hopes and their dreams. We talked about their aspirations. See, because many of these girls have faced unthinkable obstacles just to attend school, jeopardizing their personal safety, their freedom, risking the rejection of their families and communities.

So I thought it would be important to remind these young women how valuable and precious they are. I wanted them to understand that the measure of any society is how it treats its women and girls. And I told them that they deserve to be treated with dignity and respect, and I told them that they should disregard anyone who demeans or devalues them, and that they should make their voices heard in the world. And I walked away feeling so inspired, just like I'm inspired by all the young people here – and I was so uplifted by these girls. That was Tuesday.

And now, here I am, out on the campaign trail in an election where we have consistently been hearing hurtful, hateful language about women – language that has been painful for so many of us, not just as women, but as parents trying to protect our children and raise them to be caring, respectful adults, and as citizens who think that our nation's leaders should meet basic standards of human decency.

The fact is that in this election, we have a candidate for president of the United States who, over the course of his lifetime and the course of this campaign, has said things about women that are so shocking, so demeaning that I simply will not repeat anything here today. And last week, we saw this candidate actually bragging about

CHAPTER 12

"This government should give us everything we need in the form of machinery., material, and finance. Enough to last for twenty to twenty-five years until we can become an independent people and an independent nation in our own land."
—Malcom X.

On our land we do not wish to be segregated. It isn't our goal to stay away from other races. We just want to control our community.

Malcom X once said these words, Words we plan to take into the future with us.

"A segregated district or community is a community in which people live, but out siders control the politics and the economy and the community.

They never refer to the white section as a segregated community. It's the all-negro section that's a segregated community. Why? The white man controls his schools, his own banks, his own economy, his own politics, his own everything, his own community, but he also controls yours.

When you're under someone else's control you're segregated. They'll always give you the lowest or the worst there is to offer, but that doesn't mean you're segregated just because you have your own. You've got to control your own. Just like the white man has control of his, you need to control yours."

Those words are true, and we really believe that is the way to go. Even if people call us all kinds of names, we can't let that get in our way. Sometimes you've got

sexually assaulting women. And I can't believe that I'm saying that a candidate for president of the United States has bragged about sexually assaulting women.

And I have to tell you that I can't stop thinking about this. It has shaken me to my core in a way that I couldn't have predicted. So while I'd love nothing more than to pretend like this isn't happening, and to come out here and do my normal campaign speech, it would be dishonest and disingenuous of me to just move on to the next thing like this was all just a bad dream.

This is not something that we can ignore. It's not something we can just sweep under the rug as just another disturbing footnote in a sad election season. Because this was not just a "lewd conversation". This wasn't just locker-room banter. This was a powerful individual speaking freely and openly about sexually predatory behavior, and actually bragging about kissing and groping women, using language so obscene that many of us were worried about our children hearing it when we turn on the TV.

And to make matters worse, it now seems very clear that this isn't an isolated incident. It's one of countless examples of how he has treated women his whole life. And I have to tell you that I listen to all of this and I feel it so personally, and I'm sure that many of you do too, particularly the women. The shameful comments about our bodies. The disrespect of our ambitions and intellect. The belief that you can do anything you want to a woman.

It is cruel. It's frightening. And the truth is, it hurts. It hurts. It's like that sick, sinking feeling you get when you're walking down the street minding your own business and some guy yells out vulgar words about your body. Or when you see

to say who gives a fuck to what people say about us.

I can care less what none members think about us if we're making our members happy. When you're trying to change the world, you won't please everybody.

So, when the haters say we want segregation, well say we just want a place to call ours. A place that's a beacon of light and hope for millions of Pride members, and people who have been seared in the flames of injustice. A place that will end the long years of captivity.

Rich Pride and its black state should be free and independent with the sight to have full power to make war, conclude peace, and to do all the acts and things which other states may do.

We understand what will be said about us to deceive the American people. But we don't care, we are doing our duty by stating our views.

We proclaim the rights of our people to be free. We want for them what's rightly theirs: wealth, natural resources, we stand for the aspirations of our people.

That's where we stand, we stand for all that is just: we condemn starvation wages for our teachers, we condemn discrimination against any race, we condemn the inequality and exploitation of women, we condemn any government which ignores the demands of some of their people.

In short Rich Pride condemns the exploitation of man by man, and the exploitation of underdeveloped countries.

We proclaim to our members the right for us to own our own land as people.

that guy at work that stands just a little too close, stares a little too long, and makes you feel uncomfortable in your own skin.

It's that feeling of terror and violation that too many women have felt when someone has grabbed them, or forced himself on them and they've said no but he didn't listen – something that we know happens on college campuses and countless other places every single day. It reminds us of stories we heard from our mothers and grandmothers about how, back in their day, the boss could say and do whatever he pleased to the women in the office, and even though they worked so hard, jumped over every hurdle to prove themselves, it was never enough.

We thought all of that was ancient history, didn't we? And so many have worked for so many years to end this kind of violence and abuse and disrespect, but here we are in 2016 and we're hearing these exact same things every day on the campaign trail. We are drowning in it. And all of us are doing what women have always done: we're trying to keep our heads above water, just trying to get through it, trying to pretend like this doesn't really bother us maybe because we think that admitting how much it hurts makes us as women look weak.

Maybe we're afraid to be that vulnerable. Maybe we've grown accustomed to swallowing these emotions and staying quiet, because we've seen that people often won't take our word over his. Or maybe we don't want to believe that there are still people out there who think so little of us as women. Too many are treating this as just another day's headline, as if our outrage is overblown or unwarranted, as if this is normal, just politics as usual.

But, New Hampshire, be clear: this is not

We take on Martin Luther King dream in some form, we take on Malcom X wishes and combine them into something revolutionary for the black race.

We stand here today reminding the black race of the fire urgency of "now."

Now is the time to lift our people from the quicksand of racial injustice to the solid rock of brotherhood.

It would be fatal for us to overlook the urgency of now.

There are people who will ask us "when will we be satisfied?"

To which we will answer with the words of Martin Luther King, "We can never be satisfied as long as the negro is a victim of the unspeakable horrors of police brutality."

We can never be satisfied until we end poverty for the black race.

That is our main goal, and we will spend the rest of our lives working on plans to change this.

Because of poverty, people are dying from gang wars over drugs. Our people are killing each other to move "work" on corners trying to get out of poverty.

We need to end the hunger in the black community, because that's what's pushing most drug dealers into the business.

This must change because constant excuses for inaction no longer do, they are no longer any good. We must be passionate about change. We must be organized to change this world for our kids.

What I'm asking and what I'm saying is not that complicated. If we love our kids, our people, and care about getting ahead, and the future, then it should be

normal. This is not politics as usual. This is disgraceful. It is intolerable. And it doesn't matter what party you belong to – Democrat, Republican, independent – no woman deserves to be treated this way. None of us deserves this kind of abuse. And I know it's a campaign, but this isn't about politics. It's about basic human decency. It's about right and wrong.

And we simply cannot endure this, or expose our children to this any – not for another minute, and let alone for four years. Now is the time for all of us to stand up and say enough is enough. This has got to stop right now.

Because consider this: if all of this is painful to us as grown women, what do you think this is doing to our children? What message are our little girls hearing about who they should look like, how they should act? What lessons are they learning about their value as professionals, as human beings, about their dreams and aspirations? And how is this affecting men and boys in this country? Because I can tell you that the men in my life do not talk about women like this. And I know that my family is not unusual. And to dismiss this as everyday locker-room talk is an insult to decent men everywhere.

The men that you and I know don't treat women this way. They are loving fathers who are sickened by the thought of their daughters being exposed to this kind of vicious language about women. They are husbands and brothers and sons who don't tolerate women being treated and demeaned and disrespected. And like us, these men are worried about the impact this election is having on our boys who are looking for role models of what it means to be a man.

In fact, someone recently told me a story about their six-year-

easy to find the courage to come together.

We can find the courage to get mobilized and organized. We can find the courage to cut through the noise of the naysayers and do what any sensible people would do. That's what we're trying to do. And what every black person should be trying to do tomorrow. And if they do, they will leave behind a race that's stronger than the one we inherited, and one that is worthy of young people willing to fight for everything they deserve.

It is an honor for me to write this first book "Rich Pride." It will be remembered as one of the greatest moments of my life.

Just writing it inspires me to take action. And I plan on spending the rest of my life serving my people, and anyway possible.

I will fight to end poverty for all blacks, not just Americans. But it will begin here in America to begin giving blacks their share of wealth.

In Nelson Mandela's words "I stand here before you not as a prophet, but as a humble servant of you the people. Your tireless and heroic sacrifices have made it possible for me to be here today. I therefore place the remaining years of my life in your hands."

I know we haven't achieved much, but one day we will, and until that day the rest of my life, I will help my people.

old son who one day was watching the news – they were watching the news together. And the little boy, out of the blue, said, "I think Hillary Clinton will be president." And his mom said, "Well, why do you say that?" And this little six-year-old said, "Because the other guy called someone a piggy and," he said, "You cannot be president if you call someone a piggy."

So even a six-year-old knows better. A six-year-old knows that this is not how adults behave. This is not how decent human beings behave. And this is certainly not how someone who wants to be president of the United States behaves.

Because let's be very clear: strong men – men who are truly role models – don't need to put down women to make themselves feel powerful. People who are truly strong lift others up. People who are truly powerful bring others together. And that is what we need in our next president. We need someone who is a uniting force in this country. We need someone who will heal the wounds that divide us, someone who truly cares about us and our children, someone with strength and compassion to lead this country forward.

And let me tell you, I'm here today because I believe with all of my heart that Hillary Clinton will be that president.

See, we know that Hillary is the right person for the job because we've seen her character and commitment not just in this campaign, but over the course of her entire life. The fact is that Hillary embodies so many of the values that we try so hard to teach our young people. We tell our young people "work hard in school, get a good education". We encourage them to use that education to help others – which is exactly what Hillary did with her college and law degrees, advocating for

CHAPTER 13

"After four hundred years of slave labor, we have some back pay coming, a bill is owed to us and must be collected."
—Malcom X.

Over a century ago, Washington laid the cornerstone of the capital in what was then little more than wooded wilderness.

To build our community from the ground up, that's where things will have to start for us. We will need time before it is necessary to provide great buildings for our businesses, and for our government. With time things will grow and our need for housing our government will be met. We will have a growth of wealth and a growth in complex interest.

The weak-minded won't be able to take a stand and go without things they feel is necessary, and to those people we say, stand strong and give it a try, give us a try. Our community will come together. We will build a big city that's our own. I call on my people to think about how slaves live life, to remember the people who really went without being noticed. Slaves were the ones who had nothing to look forward to, their dreams didn't have a chance of fulfilment, they live life almost hopeless. They had real problems. But even with the world against them, they still tried to live a meaningful life, even with hopeless dreams they still dreamed, and sometimes give their lives for these hopeless dreams.

When I think about them, it makes me believe it's nothing for us to follow ours. On our land we

kids with disabilities, fighting for children's healthcare as first lady, affordable childcare in the Senate.

We teach our kids the value of being a team player, which is what Hillary exemplified when she lost the 2008 election and actually agreed to work for her opponent as our secretary of state – earning sky-high approval ratings serving her country once again.

We also teach our kids that you don't take shortcuts in life, and you strive for meaningful success in whatever job you do. Well, Hillary has been a lawyer, a law professor, first lady of Arkansas, first lady of the United States, a US senator, secretary of state. And she has been successful in every role, gaining more experience and exposure to the presidency than any candidate in our lifetime – more than Barack, more than Bill. And, yes, she happens to be a woman.

And finally, we teach our kids that when you hit challenges in life, you don't give up, you stick with it. Well, during her four years as secretary of state alone, Hillary has faced her share of challenges. She's traveled to 112 countries, negotiated a ceasefire, a peace agreement, a release of dissidents. She spent 11 hours testifying before a congressional committee. We know that when things get tough, Hillary doesn't complain. She doesn't blame others. She doesn't abandon ship for something easier. No, Hillary Clinton has never quit on anything in her life

So in Hillary, we have a candidate who has dedicated her life to public service, someone who has waited her turn and helped out while waiting. She is an outstanding mother. She has raised a phenomenal young woman. She is a loving, loyal wife. She's a devoted daughter who cared for her mother

will have a tough time coming up with the money to build our infrastructure, we might have to live out of tents until we have the money to build houses.

But they will have the best tents available. We will live the best life we could, it won't be the best life there is, but it will be the beginning of our independence.

We may start off going from pay day to pay day, just like millions of others, but it won't be for long. The day will come where everyone will have decent incomes and won't have to worry. How they will pay the rising car insurance bill or any other bill.

The day will come where we will fly our flag on our land and we will walk alone trying to make it better for ourselves and our children.

I ask people to think about the power of trying and where a new idea can take you.

In 1894, a New York Times writer warned against the dangers of riding a bicycle, predicting that it would lead to "weakness of the mind, general lunacy, and homicidal maniac."

In 1925, the Dean of Princeton University asserted that cars would make young people "look lightly at moral code."

These are two fucked up predictions. People need to understand that innovation isn't as scary as it seems. I remember these predictions anytime I confuse "new" with "threatening."

What we're building is important. A project like this we will learn new skills. I don't care if there is no foreseeable payoff right now, all that matters is the betterment of my people.

until her final days. And if any of us had raised a daughter like Hillary Clinton, we would be so proud. We would be proud. And regardless of who her opponent might be, no one could be more qualified for this job than Hillary – no one. And in this election, if we turn away from her, if we just stand by and allow her opponent to be elected, then what are we teaching our children about the values they should hold, about the kind of life they should lead? What are we saying?

In our hearts, we all know that if we let Hillary's opponent win this election, then we are sending a clear message to our kids that everything they're seeing and hearing is perfectly OK. We are validating it. We are endorsing it. We're telling our sons that it's OK to humiliate women. We're telling our daughters that this is how they deserve to be treated. We're telling all our kids that bigotry and bullying are perfectly acceptable in the leader of their country. Is that what we want for our children?And remember, we won't just be setting a bad example for our kids, but for our entire world. Because for so long, America has been a model for countries across the globe, pushing them to educate their girls, insisting that they give more rights to their women. But if we have a president who routinely degrades women, who brags about sexually assaulting women, then how can we maintain our moral authority in the world? How can we continue to be a beacon of freedom and justice and human dignity?

Well, fortunately, New Hampshire, here's the beauty: we have everything we need to stop this madness. You see, while our mothers and grandmothers were often powerless to change their circumstances, today, we as women have all the power we need to

Right now, I'm trying to build a team that will help Rich Pride reach our target audience. We want smart people on our team, because when you learn how smart people think, we all get smarter. What I want my people to take from the power of trying is we need to take chances.

Some people want to know how time invested will lead to a direct payout, and I understand that. But one of the facts of life is we'll never know exactly how, when, or why something we do will pay off.

Our life and business aren't straight lines; they aren't predictable or perfectly controllable. They're simply a series of opportunities — and when a great one comes along, we need to be able to say, "let's give it a shot."

We should always try, because there are so many opportunities we could miss being scared of trying.

That's why we all should jump into projects like this, even if we don't know how, or, if it'll pay off. Rich Pride members need to play the long game. The future is unknowable, full of challenges and potential.

But I do know this: The more wisely we spend our time today, the more we take risks, and search for new passions, and figure out new things as we stumble around in the dark. We'll become better, smarter, and satisfied tomorrow.

When we have our own land, it won't be everything we wish for it to be right away, but it will be ours. This vision will take time and our members need to believe and invest in our future.

determine the outcome of this election.

We have knowledge. We have a voice. We have a vote. And on November the 8th, we as women, we as Americans, we as decent human beings can come together and declare that enough is enough, and we do not tolerate this kind of behavior in this country.

Remember this: in 2012, women's votes were the difference between Barack winning and losing in key swing states, including right here in New Hampshire. So for anyone who might be thinking that your one vote doesn't really matter, or that one person can't really make a difference, consider this: back in 2012, Barack won New Hampshire by about 40,000 votes, which sounds like a lot. But when you break that number down, the difference between winning and losing this state was only 66 votes per precinct. Just take that in. If 66 people in each precinct had gone the other way, Barack would have lost.

So each of you right here today could help swing an entire precinct and win this election for Hillary just by getting yourselves, your families, and your friends and neighbors out to vote. You can do it right here. But you could also help swing an entire precinct for Hillary's opponent with a protest vote or by staying home out of frustration.

Because here's the truth: either Hillary Clinton or her opponent will be elected president this year. And if you vote for someone other than Hillary, or if you don't vote at all, then you are helping to elect her opponent. And just think about how you will feel if that happens. Imagine waking up on November the 9th and looking into the eyes of your daughter or son, or looking into your own eyes as you stare into the mirror. Imagine how you'll feel if you stayed home, or if you didn't

CHAPTER 14

I know I'm no hero. The world knows about my mistakes. But I know I was never meant to play the villain. I take some solace knowing that, in the end, history will judge me and all that I have accomplished with Rich Pride will speak volumes. Perhaps children someday will read about me the way I read about Martin Luther King Jr.

Rich Pride's goal is to transform the black race from the crying cub to a roaring lion. We hope to change our days of being last. We will lead the way, join us today and make a difference. If you do there will be no turning back, know that certain realities will have to be faced. Now is the time for chess moves, greatness is hard not easy, but it is possible.

Sometimes progress can skip a generation, but we won't let it skip us. While I write this book, I feel like it has been a long time I've been thinking about change and finding a way to help my people.

I'm about to say a few words from my heart. I never wished to withhold how I feel, but until now I didn't have the drive to make it possible. I want to start by declaring my allegiance to Rich Pride, and I mean that with all my heart.

I want every person who believes in our mission and want to help declare their allegiance to our flag by becoming a member. Also, I want people to understand there will be no misrepresentation of our flag. To stop this there will be a membership process and a database to confirm membership. The decision to join Rich Pride must be yours and yours alone.

do everything possible to elect Hillary.

We simply cannot let that happen. We cannot allow ourselves to be so disgusted that we just shut off the TV and walk away. And we can't just sit around wringing our hands. Now, we need to recover from our shock and depression and do what women have always done in this country. We need you to roll up your sleeves. We need to get to work. Because remember this: When they go low, we go …

Audience: High!

Yes, we do.

And voting ourselves is a great start, but we also have to step up and start organizing. So we need you to make calls and knock on doors and get folks to the polls on election day and sign up to volunteer with one of the Hillary campaign folks who are here today just waiting for you to step up.

And, young people and not-so-young people, get on social media. Share your own story of why this election matters, why it should matter for all people of conscience in this country. There is so much at stake in this election.

See, the choice you make November 8 could determine whether we have a president who treats people with respect – or not. A president who will fight for kids, for good schools, for good jobs for our families – or not. A president who thinks that women deserve the right to make our own choices about our bodies and our health – or not. That's just a little bit of what's at stake.

So we cannot afford to be tired or turned off. And we cannot afford to stay home on election day. Because on November the 8th, we have the power to show our children that America's greatness comes from recognizing the innate dignity and worth of all our people. On November the 8th, we can show our children that this country is big

You should really be in for the long run.

I'm making this the most serious decision of my life, and I know it's what's best for me. All members should do the same, they should know what they are willing to do to help their people.

It may be sometime before I walk on land owned by Rich Pride, but I will always work to make it happen. We will build our empire. We will find happiness and prosperity.

I want it to be clear that Rich Pride seeks to establish a domination over the world completely different from any known to history.

The domination that Rich Pride seeks is not limited to the displaced man of the balance of power. We seek political and economic power over any nation in this world.

We will embrace our culture, by making it a great part of history, taking our people from being deprived means of moral and material happiness to the kings they were born. Saving our liberty and human dignity.

As I write this book all I have is blood, sweat, and tears to offer my people. But I believe and have full confidence that if all do their duty, if nothing is neglected and if the best arrangement is made, as they are being made, we shall prove ourselves willing and able to rise above poverty.

At any rate that is what Rich Pride is going to do. We will fight with growing confidence and growing strength in the air. We will never surrender our dream for prosperity.

My heart is into changing the world, and I know it's possible because I believe and the power enough to have a place for us all – men and women, folks of every background and walk of life – and that each of us is a precious part of this great American story, and we are always stronger together.

On November 8, we can show our children that here in America, we reject hatred and fear and in difficult times, we don't discard our highest ideals. No, we rise up to meet them. We rise up to perfect our union. We rise up to defend our blessings of liberty. We rise up to embody the values of equality and opportunity and sacrifice that have always made this country the greatest nation on Earth. That is who we are. And don't ever let anyone tell you differently. Hope is important. Hope is important for our young people. And we deserve a president who can see those truths in us – a president who can bring us together and bring out the very best in us. Hillary Clinton will be that president. So for the next 26 days, we need to do everything we can to help her and Tim Kaine win this election. I know I'm going to be doing it. Are you with me? Are you all with me? You ready to roll up your sleeves? Get to work knocking on doors?All right, let's get to work. Thank you all. God bless.

Michelle Obama is a strong woman and I really, respect her. She can't do anything wrong in my eyes! She's smart, beautiful, and a inspiration to people all around the world. I agree with everything she said about woman in the way they should be treated, they are valuable in precious, but that's not the way they are treated in the black community. Now don't get me wrong there are black men in our community who treat our woman with respect. But on the other hand, I've had conversations with man who believe there is nothing wrong with what Trump said. They

of being together, and I believe in my people. A movement is taking place and every man, and woman who wants change needs to do more and say less. Change won't come if it's only bitched about. It takes action if you have the privilege to read this book, it's a call to action. I say if you have the privilege because only 20 of these will exist. If you are one of the people to lay your hands on a copy, I ask that you only share it with someone you believe want to make a difference.

Pride: primary reviving investment decision economically.

Rich Pride we will not be paralyzed by fear, we will be energized by it.

RICH PRIDE DECLARATION OF INDEPENDENCE

When in the course of human events, it becomes necessary for one people to dissolve the political bond which have connected them with another, and to assume among the power of the earth, the separate in equal station to which the laws of nature and of nature's god entitle them, a decent respect to the opinions of mankind requires that they should declare the causes which impel them to the separation. We hold these truths to be self-evident, that all men are created equal, that they are endowed by their creator with certain unalienable rights, that among these are life, liberty, and the pursuit of happiness that to secure these rights, government are instituted among men, deriving their just powers from the consent of the believe things like this happen everyday in the "hood." In it's true, but to them I say, just because the woman didn't call the police on you, don't mean your not sexually assaulting her. When I say this, their face screw up, because sexual assault is something to be ashamed about in the hood. They all are quick to say it's not sexual assault, but it is! Michelle Obama said something that I will never forget, she said "The measure of any society is how they treat its woman and girls." She went on to say that woman deserve to be treated with dignity and respect.

We the people of Rich Pride share her vision, we don't care if they are strippers, prostitutes, or business woman, if they join Rich Pride, they will belong to an organization, where they are treated with respect. They will join a nation where they are treated and paid the same as males.

OBAMA: Hey! (Applause.) What's going on? (Applause.) Thank you all so much. You guys, that's a command — rest yourselves. (Laughter.) We're almost at the end. (Laughter.) Hello, everyone. And, may I say for the last time officially, welcome to the White House. Yes! (Applause.) Well, we are beyond thrilled to have you all here to celebrate the 2017 National School Counselor of the Year, as well as all of our State Counselors of the Year. These are the fine women, and a few good men — (laughter) — one good man — who are on this stage, and they represent schools from across this country.

And I want to start by thanking Terri for that wonderful introduction and her right-on-the-spot remarks. I'm going to say a lot more about Terri in a few minutes,

governed, that whenever any form of government becomes destructive to these ends, it is the right of the people to alter or to abolish it, and to institute new government, laying its foundation on such principles, and organizing its powers in such form, as to them shall seem most likely to affect their safety and happiness. Prudence, indeed, will dictate that governments long established should not be changed for light and transient causes; and accordingly, all experience hath shewn, that mankind is more disposed to suffer, while evils are sufferable, than to right themselves to abolishing the form to which they are accustomed. But when along train of abuses and usurpations, pursuing invariably the same object, evinces a design to reduce them under absolute despotism. it is their right, it is their duty, to throw off such government, and to provide new guards for their future security. Such has been the patient sufferance of the Black race; and such is now the necessity which constrain them to alter their former systems of government. The history of the United States of America is a history of repeated injuries to the black race, all having in direct object the establishment of an absolute tyranny over black people. To prove this, let facts be submitted to the candid world.

Slavery in the United States was a legal institution of human chattel enslavement, primarily of Africans and African Americans that existed in the United states of America in the 18th and 19th centuries. 300 years later we are free but being gunned down every day. The city of Ferguson, Missouri was a flashpoint for protest since the killing of an unarmed black teenager by a

but first I want to take a moment to acknowledge a few people who are here.

First, our outstanding Secretary of Education, John King. (Applause.) As well as our former Education Secretary, Arne Duncan. (Applause.) I want to take this time to thank you both publicly for your dedication and leadership and friendship. We couldn't do this without the support of the Department of Education under both of your leadership. So, I'm grateful to you personally, and very proud of all that you've done for this country. I also want to acknowledge a few other special guests we have in the audience. We've got a pretty awesome crew. As one of my staff said, "You roll pretty deep." (Laughter.) I'm like, well, yeah, we have a few good friends. We have with us today Ted Allen, La La Anthony, Connie Britton, Andy Cohen — yeah, Andy Cohen is here — (laughter) — Carla Hall, Coach Jim Harbaugh and his beautiful wife, who's a lot better looking than him — (laughter) — Lana Parrilla, my buddy Jay Pharoah, Kelly Rowland, Usher — AUDIENCE MEMBER: Woo!

MRS. OBAMA: Keep it down. (Laughter.) Keep it together, ladies. Wale is here. And of course, Allison <u>Williams</u> and her mom are here.

And all these folks are here because they're using their star power to inspire our young people. And I'm so grateful to all of you for stepping up in so many ways on so many occasions. I feel like I've pestered you over these years, asking time and time again, "Well, where are you going to be?" "I'm going to be in New York." "Can you come? Can you come here? Can you do this? Can you take that? Can you ask for that? Can you come? Can we rap? Can we sing?" (Laughter.) So thank you all so much. It really means the

white police officer. Michael Brown was killed, and a grand jury declined to charge the officer with murder. A justice department investigation found widespread racial bias in the police force. Initially, these demonstrations focus on Ferguson, but they spread to other U.S cities after the jury decided not to charge the officer, Darren Wilson. Mr. Wilson was a white officer and Mr. Brown was a black teenager. We see this case as a case of racism and police brutality. The police brutality to blacks don't stop there, the U.S Department of Justice has decided to charge white officers who shot and killed Alton Sterling. Another case is Philand castile who was killed when he was asked to get his license. The officer in this case said, "He had no other option but to shoot." A series of fatal police shooting involving African -Americans has sparked a debate about police use of force against blacks. These cases show an unwillingness to prosecute. The decision not to prosecute is making a highly toxic environment, defined by decades of bad feeling spurred by illegal-and-misguided practices. So, as you can see, it is not difficult to imagine how these tragic incidents set off city like powder kegs. The federal decision to not prosecute most of these cases is all the reason in the world to ask for independences. The black race is not getting closure, we are not getting justice. There is a war being fought with only one side being able to legally kill. There is a racial bias in the U.S Government, and it's time we say, "no more." In every stage of our oppression we have petitioned and the humblest terms. Our repeated petitions have been answered only by repeated injury. We have a president

world to this initiative to have such powerful, respected and admired individuals speaking on behalf of this issue. So congratulations on the work that you've done, and we're going to keep working.

And today, I especially want to recognize all these — extraordinary leadership team that was behind Reach Higher from day one. And this isn't on the script so they don't know this. I want to take time to personally acknowledge a couple of people. Executive Director Eric Waldo. (Applause.) Where is Eric? He's in the — you've got to step out. (Applause.) Eric is acting like he's a ham, but he likes the spotlight. (Laughter.) He's acting a little shy. I want to recognize our Deputy Director, Stephanie Sprow. Stephanie. (Applause.) And he's really not going to like this because he tries to pretend like he doesn't exist at all, but our Senior Advisor, Greg Darnieder. (Applause.) There you go. Greg has been a leader in education his entire life. I've known him since I was a little organizer person. And it's just been just a joy to work with you all. These individuals, they are brilliant. They are creative. They have worked miracles with hardly any staff or budget to speak of — which is how we roll in the First Lady's Office. (Laughter.) And I am so proud and so, so grateful to you all for everything that you've done. So let's give them a round of applause. (Applause.)

And finally, I want to recognize all of you who are here in this audience. We have our educators, our leaders, our young people who have been with us since we launched Reach Higher back in 2014. Now, when we first came up with this idea, we had one clear goal in mind: We wanted to make higher education cool. We wanted to change the conversation around what it means and what it takes to

whose character is thus marked by every act which may define a tyrant and he is unfit to be the president of a free people. We must, there for declaration, that all members of Rich Pride have the right and ought to be free and independent; that they are absolved from all allegiance to the U.S government and ought to be totally dissolved; and that as free and independent state, they have the full power to levy war, conclude peace, contract alliances, establish commerce, and to do all other acts and things which independent states may do. For the protection of divine providence, we mutually pledge to each other our lives, fortunes and our sacred honor.

RICH PRIDE GOVERNMENT

EXECUTIVE BRANCH

President

Vice President

Security Council

Office of Management and Budget

Office of Drug Control Policy

Office of Science and technology

Office of Chief of Staff

Office of Digital Strategy

Office of Public Engagement

CABINET DEPARTMENT HEADS

Secretary of State

Secretary of the Treasure

Secretary of Defense

Secretary of Labor

be a success in this country. Because let's be honest, if we're always shining the spotlight on professional athletes or recording artists or Hollywood celebrities, if those are the only achievements we celebrate, then why would we ever think kids would see college as a priority? So we decided to flip the script and shine a big, bright spotlight on all things educational. For example, we made College Signing Day a national event. We wanted to mimic all the drama and excitement traditionally reserved for those few amazing football and basketball players choosing their college and university teams. We wanted to focus that same level of energy and attention on kids going to college because of their academic achievements. Because as a nation, that's where the spotlight should also be — on kids who work hard in school and do the right thing when no one is watching, many beating daunting odds.

Next, we launched Better Make Room. It's a social media campaign to give young people the support and inspiration they need to actually complete higher education. And to really drive that message home, you may recall that I debuted my music career — (laughter) — rapping with Jay about getting some knowledge by going to college. (Laughter and applause.)

We are also very proud of all that this administration has done to make higher education more affordable. We doubled investments in Pell grants and college tax credits. We expanded income-based loan repayment options for tens of millions of students. We made it easier to apply for financial aid. We created a College Scorecard to help students make good decisions about higher education. And we provided new funding and support for school counselors. (Applause.) Altogether,

Secretary of Health and Human Services

Secretary of housing and Urban Development

Secretary of Energy

Secretary of Education

EXECUTIVE OFFICE

Office of Management and Budget

Office of Science and Technology Policy

Office of the Director of Intelligence

PRESIDENT STAFF

Chief of Staff

Deputy Chief of Staff

Deputy Chief of Staff for Operations

Senior Counselor

Senior Adviser

Cabinet Secretary

Adviser to the President

Counsel to the President

Press secretary

Security Adviser

Director of Communications

Director of Political Affairs

Director of Social Media

THE CABINET

The head of major executive department of the Rich Pride Government constitute the cabinet. This institution is an advisory body for the desire of the president to consult on policy matters. Aside from its advisory role, the cabinet has no formal function and no executive authority. Individual members exercise authority as heads of their departments, reporting to

we made in this administration the largest investment in higher education since the G.I. Bill. (Applause.) And today, the high school graduation rate is at a record high, and more young people than ever before are going to college.

And we know that school counselors like all of the folks standing with me on this stage have played a critical role in helping us get there. In fact, a recent study showed that students who met with a school counselor to talk about financial aid or college were three times more likely to attend college, and they were nearly seven times more likely to apply for financial aid.

So our school counselors are truly among the heroes of the Reach Higher story. And that's why we created this event two years ago, because we thought that they should finally get some recognition. (Applause.) We wanted everyone to know about the difference that these phenomenal men and women have been making in the lives of our young people every day. And our 2017 School Counselor of the Year, Terri Tchorzynski, is a perfect example.

As you heard, Terri works at the Calhoun Area Career Center, a career and technical education school in Michigan. And here's what Terri's principal said about her in his letter of recommendation. He said, "Once she identifies a systemic need, she works tirelessly to address it."

So when students at Terri's school reported feeling unprepared to apply for higher education, Terri sprang into action to create a school-wide, top-to-bottom college-readiness effort. Under Terri's leadership, more students than ever before attended workshops on resume writing, FAFSA completion — yes, I can now say FAFSA — (laughter) — and

the president. They meet at times set by the president.

Cabinet-level Department, secretaries

DEPARTMENT OF STATE

The Foreign Service protects Rich Pride members and interests. They maintain contact with foreign governments, negotiates agreement and treaties, and supports Rich Pride foreign trade.

DEPARTMENT OF TREASURY

They are responsible for the fiscal affairs of Rich Pride. It serves as the government's financial agent; collects, borrows, and disburses funds for the government. Monitors the finical infrastructure and economic development; recommends domestic and international financial, monetary, economic, trade, and tax policies. Manufactures currency and coins.

DEPARTMENT OF DEFENSE

They direct and control the armed forces and assists the president in protecting the nation's security. They conduct military operations and is the principal military adviser to the president.

DEPARTMENT OF ENERGY

Secures the nation's energy and promotes scientific and technological innovation.

DEPARTMENT OF EDUCATION

Conducts research and gathers educational information to disseminate to educators and the general public.

interview preparation. I can barely say it. (Laughter.) They did career and personal — personality assessments. They helped plan a special college week. And they organized a Military Day, hosting recruiters from all branches of our armed forces. And because of these efforts, today, 75 percent of Calhoun's seniors now complete key college application steps, and Terri's school has won state and national recognition.

And all of this is just one small part of what Terri does for her students each day. I can go on and on about all the time she spends one-on-one with students, helping them figure out their life path. Terri told us — as you heard, she told us about one of those students, so we reached out to Kyra. And here's what Kyra had to say in her own words. Kyra wrote that "Mrs. Tchorzynski has helped me grow to love myself. She helped me with my doubts and insecurities." She said, my life has changed "for the better in all aspects." Kyra said, "She held my hand through my hardest times." She said, "Mrs. Tchorzynski is my lifesaver." That's what Kyra said. (Laughter.)

And this is what each of you do every single day. You see the promise in each of your students. You believe in them even when they can't believe in themselves, and you work tirelessly to help them be who they were truly meant to be. And you do it all in the face of some overwhelming challenges — tight budgets, impossible student- counselor ratios — yeah, amen — (laughter) — endless demands on your time.

You all come in early, you stay late. You reach into your own pockets — and see, we've got the amen corner. (Laughter.) You stick with students in their darkest moments, when they're most anxious and afraid. And if anyone is dealing with a college [high school] senior or junior, you

Lions are known to many as the top of the food chain and the most dominant force in the African bush. Male lions are viewed as a majestic creature, a protector, a father, warrior, and a soldier. A male lion will put his life on the line for his pride, for his females, and his young. They will sacrifice anything for the greater good of their land and the lions upon that land. The lion dominion, power, African roots and its willingness to fight and to protect the members of his pride is the reason we choose it as the seal of Rich Pride. A pride of lions is a family like the members of Rich Pride. Just like a lion has an important role of defending the Pride, members of Rich Pride must do the same. We are willing to put our bodies on the line to defend everything that is ours. The power and the lion's ability to come together, for the greater good of all the lions that play apart in their community is a motivation for the future of our people. Over time, male lions have developed beautiful manes that serve and protect the most vital part of their body, around the neck and the head. The members of Rich Pride armed forces will have the "option" to grow locks as a sign of a male lion's power. The lionesses are also powerful, and strong like the women of Rich Pride. They are able to provide for themselves and their family. A lioness represents woman's empowerment to the members of Rich Pride. The lion also symbolizes the game of survival

know what this feels like. These men and women show them that those kids matter; that they have something to offer; that no matter where they're from or how much money their parents have, no matter what they look like or who they love or how they worship or what language they speak at home, they have a place in this country.

And as I end my time in the White House, I can think of no better message to send our young people in my last official remarks as First Lady. So for all the young people in this room and those who are watching, know that this country belongs to you — to all of you, from every background and walk of life. If you or your parents are immigrants, know that you are part of a proud American tradition — the infusion of new cultures, talents and ideas, generation after generation, that has made us the greatest country on earth.

If your family doesn't have much money, I want you to remember that in this country, plenty of folks, including me and my husband — we started out with very little. But with a lot of hard work and a good education, anything is possible — even becoming President. That's what the American Dream is all about. (Applause.)

If you are a person of faith, know that religious diversity is a great American tradition, too. In fact, that's why people first came to this country — to worship freely. And whether you are Muslim, Christian, Jewish, Hindu, Sikh — these religions are teaching our young people about justice, and compassion, and honesty. So I want our young people to continue to learn and practice those values with pride. You see, our glorious diversity — our diversities of faiths and colors and creeds — that is not a threat to the black man has faced for 400 years, where they learned that only the strongest will prevail, where we learned that if we can't provide for ourselves we will spend a lifetime in poverty. It symbolizes the confidence and growing strength in the air, and that we will never surrender our dream to transform the black race from a crying cub to a roaring lion.

First Flag	**Current Flag**

The first flag of Rich Pride had two black sides in a white middle, with a five-point star, that had a solider inside. The flag was changed and the five-point star and solider was removed because of its controversial use by gangs. The black and white stripes remain to represent the oppression of the black race by whites. One black stripe represents the ancient slavery and the other represents modern slavery.

who we are, it makes us who we are. (Applause.)

So the young people here and the young people out there: Do not ever let anyone make you feel like you don't matter, or like you don't have a place in our American story — because you do. And you have a right to be exactly who you are. But I also want to be very clear: This right isn't just handed to you. No, this right has to be earned every single day. You cannot take your freedoms for granted. Just like generations who have come before you, you have to do your part to preserve and protect those freedoms. And that starts right now, when you're young.

Right now, you need to be preparing yourself to add your voice to our national conversation. You need to prepare yourself to be informed and engaged as a citizen, to serve and to lead, to stand up for our proud American values and to honor them in your daily lives. And that means getting the best education possible so you can think critically, so you can express yourself clearly, so you can get a good job and support yourself and your family, so you can be a positive force in your communities.

And when you encounter obstacles — because I guarantee you, you will, and many of you already have — when you are struggling and you start thinking about giving up, I want you to remember something that my husband and I have talked about since we first started this journey nearly a decade ago, something that has carried us through every moment in this White House and every moment of our lives, and that is the power of hope — the belief that something better is always possible if you're willing to work for it and fight for it.

It is our fundamental belief in the power of hope that has allowed us to rise above the voices of doubt and

BLACK NATIONAL ANTHEM

Lift every voice and sing, till earth and heaven ring,

Ring with the harmonies of liberty;

Let our rejoicing rise, high as the listening skies,

Let it resound loud as the rolling sea.

Sing a song full of faith that the dark past has taught us,

Sing a song full of hope that the present has brought us;

Facing the rising sun of our new day begun,

Let us march on till victory is won.

Stony the road we trod, bitter the
chastening rod,

Felt in the days when hope
unborn had died;

Yet with a steady beat, have not
our weary feet,

Come to the place for which our
fathers sighed?

We have come over a way that
with tears has been watered,

We have come, treading our
path through the blood of the
slaughtered;

Out from the gloomy past, till
now we stand at last

Where the white gleam of our
bright star is cast.

God of our weary years, God of
our silent tears,

Thou who has brought us thus far
on the way;

division, of anger and
fear that we have faced
in our own lives and in
the life of this country.
Our hope that if we
work hard enough and
believe in ourselves,
then we can be whatever
we dream, regardless
of the limitations that
others may place on
us. The hope that when
people see us for who
we truly are, maybe, just
maybe they, too, will be
inspired to rise to their
best possible selves.

That is the hope of
students like Kyra
who fight to discover
their gifts and share
them with the world.
It's the hope of school
counselors like Terri
and all these folks up
here who guide those
students every step of
the way, refusing to
give up on even a single
young person. Shoot,
it's the hope of my —
folks like my dad who
got up every day to do
his job at the city water
plant; the hope that
one day, his kids would
go to college and have
opportunities he never
dreamed of.

That's the kind of hope that every single one of us — politicians, parents, preachers — all of us need to be providing for our young people. Because that is what moves this country forward every single day — our hope for the future and the hard work that hope inspires.

So that's my final message to young people as First Lady. It is simple. (Applause.) I want our young people to know that they matter, that they belong. So don't be afraid — you hear me, young people? Don't be afraid. Be focused. Be determined. Be hopeful. Be empowered. Empower yourselves with a good education, then get out there and use that education to build a country worthy of your boundless promise. Lead by example with hope, never fear. And know that I will be with you, rooting for you and working to support you for the rest of my life.

And that is true I know for every person who are here — is here today,

Thou who hast by Thy might, led us into the light,

Keep us forever in the path, we pray.

Lest our feet stray from the places, our God, where we met Thee,

Lest our hearts, drunk with the wine of the world, we forget Thee.

Shadowed beneath Thy hand, may we forever stand,

True to our God, true to our native land.

PRESIDENTIAL OATH OF OFFICE

The president should take the following oath. "I swear that I will faithfully execute the office of president of Rich Pride. And will, to the best of my ability, persevere, protect and defend the members of the Pride."

FOUNDER

M.L.Moore

BIBLIOGRAPHY

Malcom-X.org

Times.com

Wikipedia

20 million black people in a political, economic, in mental prison.

Politicalticker.blogs

www.theguardian.com

https://kinginstitute.stanford.edu/king-papers/documents/i-have-dream-address-delivered-march-washington-jobs-and-freedo

and for educators and advocates all across this nation who get up every day and work their hearts out to lift up our young people. And I am so grateful to all of you for your passion and your dedication and all the hard work on behalf of our next generation. And I can think of no better way to end my time as First Lady than celebrating with all of you.

So I want to close today by simply saying thank you. Thank you for everything you do for our kids and for our country. Being your First Lady has been the greatest honor of my life, and I hope I've made you proud.

Michelle really understands how important education is for our children. We want to help make education cool again, in we wish for our children to attend school all year around.